Mail Order Hope

Book Four of
Mail Order Bluebonnet Brides

Charlotte Dearing

This is a clean, wholesome love story set in late 19th century Texas. The hero is strong, successful, and flawed, in ways he doesn't realize until he meets the heroine. In the end, my heroes and heroines find a path to happiness through perseverance and faith.

This is the story of Hope, the third and youngest of the O'Brian sisters. The story stands alone, and doesn't depend on prior books in the series, but you might enjoy some of the characters more if you read the Bluebonnet Brides Series in order.

Chapter One

Hope

Hope O'Brian clung to her bravery, although it was slipping fast. She was sure she'd heard footsteps behind her, but when she stopped to listen, the footsteps stopped too. Fog blanketed the quiet Boston streets. She was alone, and possibly lost. She prayed that no one followed her.

With her heart thudding in her chest, she hurried as much as she dared. She didn't want to stumble. Night had fallen since she'd left the bookshop, and the lamplights that usually dispelled the darkness illuminated not the usual landmarks, but swirling mists of fog. Pausing, she listened again. She heard nothing.

Just eerie quiet.

When she'd finished her work at the bookshop, she'd decided to take a different path home, a path through the back streets. In the last few weeks, a man had waited outside the bookshop several nights a week. He'd follow her, trying to strike up a conversation, remarking how pretty she was and why couldn't she be a little friendlier.

She hadn't told anyone about the man. She'd simply hoped he would finally give up and pursue someone else.

Holding her breath, she wondered if perhaps he hadn't ventured out on such a night. When she concluded he wasn't following, she began walking again, the fog muffling the sound of her footsteps. Oddly, the fog seemed to amplify the sound of her ragged breath.

She tried to collect her thoughts. Nothing looked familiar. Nothing. Taking a different route home had struck her as a brilliant scheme. Now a wave of panic threatened.

"I'm not lost," she said aloud, if only to comfort herself. "I refuse to be lost."

"That's the spirit, lass."

She jumped. A small shriek of fright burst from her lips. Gabriel. It had to be Gabriel. The hint of an Irish accent, a slight slur of the words, told her the voice came from Mrs. Spencer's gardener. A kindly man who loved to cut roses and make pretty arrangements for tenants of the boarding house.

"What are you doing out here?" Hope asked with a breathless laugh. "Other than serving as a guardian angel."

"Sitting a spell on the bench here."

"A bench? At night?"

"It's a bench that sits outside of O'Malley's Pub."

Suddenly Hope realized where she was.

"Oh – of course. What a relief! But why are you out here?"

She heard the scrape of his shoes rasping across the cobblestone. "Eh. The wife said if I was going to have a wee nip, I'd need to go to the pub. The pub closed a half hour ago. If I go home now, she'll know," he paused to hiccup. "That I had more than a nee wip."

"I was lost," Hope confessed. "I've been wandering for the last hour or more, probably walking in circles."

"Aye, you're in luck, then. Gabriel has come to your rescue. Let me show you the way, Miss O'Brian."

His form appeared from the depths of heavy fog, a short, stout gentleman wearing a bowler hat. He stopped in front of her and bowed gallantly. When he straightened, he swayed

2

unsteadily, and she prayed she wouldn't have to help him home to his cottage in the garden. Still, there was something to be said for the company. Gabriel was always courteous and considerate. The relief of finding him amid the impenetrable fog felt like a godsend.

Her panic ebbed. "We make a fine pair, don't we? I'm lost and you're fresh from the pub."

Gabriel burped. "I'm the perfect fellow to escort you home. You know, Mrs. Spencer don't like her girls to go out unchaperoned. She's dismissed tenants for lesser offenses."

They walked companionably through the gloom.

Hope spoke, "I have a good excuse. I had to work. If I don't work, I can't pay rent."

Suddenly, two men appeared from the mist, large hulking figures that passed without a word. The fog made everything appear more ominous. She held her breath. Her worry flickered but faded as they passed by. The fog muted their footsteps and the sounds grew more distant. Although Gabriel didn't say anything, she sensed the men had made him uneasy too.

She shivered. If she hadn't practically stumbled over Gabriel, she would have come face to face with the men on her own.

"Miss O'Brian," Gabriel grumbled good-naturedly. "I hope you don't mind me saying, I don't approve of young ladies, such as yourself, to be out walking at night all alone."

"I stayed at the bookshop a little later than I should have."

"Hmmpf."

Hope smiled at his protectiveness. It was nice to encounter such a sweet and gallant gentleman, especially on such a dismal night, even if he was a tad tipsy. "I enjoy being in the bookshop. Sometimes I don't realize the time. One day I'll have my own bookshop, and then I'll be able to read as much as I like."

"You've always got your nose in a book," he muttered. "Me and the wife see you in the garden, always with a book."

She couldn't argue with him. Nowadays she enjoyed reading more than ever.

They walked in silence until they arrived at Spencer's Boarding House for Young Ladies. When she glimpsed the sign, she let out a breath of relief. She'd been terrified, for no good reason it turned out, but that didn't matter now. Her distress gave way to a deep exhaustion. She hadn't realized how distressed she felt walking in the fog. Under the lamplight, she could make out Gabriel's frown.

"Why don't you run off to Texas and take a husband like your sisters? A pretty lass like you could pick and choose."

"I'll never travel to Texas, Gabriel. My sisters both had no end of troubles on their journeys to Texas. Grace went all that way to find her intended had passed away. The man's brother coerced her into marriage. Faith made the same trip and was duped by a bank robber."

Gabriel's jaw dropped. "A bank robber?"

"That's right. Poor girl. She agreed to take a bag to Magnolia, her destination, never dreaming it held stolen money. The sheriff greeted her at the railway station. Come to find out, the sheriff was her intended. Can you imagine?"

"Did he arrest her?"

"He married her. You could say she was duped again, this time into matrimony."

Gabriel scratched his head, swaying unsteadily. "I'm having trouble keeping up with your story."

Hope lifted her chin. "Never mind. It doesn't matter. I'll never marry. One day, I might summon the courage to visit my sisters, but only time will tell."

He nodded. "You take good care now. Boston's a nasty place after dark. Even in these parts."

She hurried inside and was greeted by her landlady, Mrs. Spencer. "You've missed supper."

"I stayed a little late at the bookshop."

The woman sat behind a desk, peering at her over her spectacles. "You've been doing that quite a bit lately. It's becoming a habit."

Hope tried her best to keep a cordial expression. The boarding house was one of the finest in Boston and Mrs. Spencer was quite proud of her reputation. But she also liked to pry into the lives of her boarders. She was strict too, and very concerned with propriety. Anyone else, and Hope might have shared the reason she needed to stay late.

Her employer, Mr. Jones, had become more and more absent-minded over the last few months. He made mistakes in the books as well as the orders. A time or two, she'd gone to check on him and found him asleep with the lamp burning.

Lately, she stayed after to correct the errors, check his work and make sure he hadn't left a candle or lamp burning. If she told Mrs. Spencer her reasons, the woman would discuss it with her friends and neighbors. Hope couldn't bear the thought that people would gossip about Mr. Jones.

"Any letters for me?" she asked, taking off her damp cloak.

Mrs. Spencer pinched her lips. "One from a Faith Bentley."

Hope took the letter and bid Mrs. Spencer goodnight. The upstairs servant greeted her at her door with a plate and a promise of hot water for a bath. At times, Hope didn't care for all of Mrs. Spencer's rules, but the girls she hired made up for her unpleasant ways.

She soaked in the tub and read Faith's letter. Hope's heart warmed to hear that Faith and her husband were expecting a child sometime in early summer. She set the letter aside and tried to tamp her feelings of loneliness. In a way, it was a blessing to have a great deal of work at the bookshop. Her extra chores kept her from missing her sisters so much.

Reflecting on the reason she couldn't visit her sisters, or at least not yet, she pursed her lips with irritation. She'd like nothing more than to go to Texas to visit her sisters, and she would have done just that if it weren't for her sisters' brother-in-law.

Lucas Bentley...

He'd written her two letters. One to tell him about himself, four pages, beginning with the fact that ladies told him he was handsome – *very* handsome. He then proceeded to list them and promised that he was the finest, most hard-working and upstanding of the Bentley brothers. He added details of his ranch and how he'd like to start a Brahma operation. He concluded the letter with a few lines of how she could hardly do worse than marry him and he figured he might as well snap up the last O'Brian sister.

"Pure poetry," she muttered as she dried off and slipped into her nightgown.

She'd written him back to tell him he was arrogant, and she wasn't interested in being snapped up. In his next letter, he explained that eventually she'd come around and see he had a fine plan.

And if that doesn't work, I might come to Boston and charm you into coming back to Texas and marrying me...

"Charming women" into marriage seemed a family trait. Matt had hoodwinked Grace into marriage just as Thomas had coerced Faith.

Her sisters might be easily fooled, but not her. Everyone knew Hope was the steady one. Which was not to say that she didn't intend to go to Texas. She simply would wait until Lucas Bentley had duped some other poor woman into marriage. Grace had written a few days ago that Lucas was keen on marrying, sooner rather than later, and once he was settled with a wife, she could ask Mr. Jones if she might take a month away from work to visit Texas. She liked to think that he was grateful for all her extra work and would allow her time to see her sisters.

By summer, she hoped to realize her dream of visiting her sisters. By that time, both sisters would have had their children. She'd be an aunt. Unimaginable. A rush of happiness came over her as she got into bed. The sheets felt like ice, but the thought of Faith and Hope starting families distracted her from the cold night.

She pushed her thoughts to Texas. In the warm months of summer, assuming Lucas had a wife and was no longer a threat, she'd travel to Texas. The idea brought a smile to her lips as she sank into her bedding. Off in the distance, the alarms of the fire brigade rang through the night. Her lids fluttered. She sat up, listened, but the piercing sounds faded.

She settled back into the pillow, her worried mind mulling over Mr. Jones's troubles. With a soft prayer, she asked God to watch over the elderly man. Aside from an older sister who dropped by the bookshop every Monday, he had no one to help him.

Sighing, she closed her eyes, let go of her worries, and drifted off to sleep.

Chapter Two

Lucas

The tail end of a dried snakeskin hung from the rafters, blowing in the breeze. The snake who previously wore this skin must have been about as big around as his forearm, Lucas Bentley thought. Fair-sized. He tugged it free and admired the length, about five feet, wondering if his eleven-year-old nephew might like the specimen. Caleb loved to collect all sorts of nature's bounty.

On the other hand, Lucas's sister-in-law wasn't much of a naturalist. Grace had made her dislike of critters pretty clear, and snakes were a particular concern for her. Lucas imagined Grace's reaction to a five-foot snakeskin draped across Caleb's bed and thought better of it.

He walked to the edge of the porch and admired the skin one last time before tossing it over the handrail. The breeze moved it a few feet and then it got stuck on some grass. He watched it for a bit, then looked up to admire the view.

Fields stretched as far as the eye could see. Miles of the best grazing pastures Lucas had ever laid eyes on. It was amazing what pastures looked like when they they'd rested for a few years. Wind blew through the vast meadows making the grass look like waves skimming across a green-gold sea.

Jim Bentley, his uncle, came to his side and eyed the snakeskin on the ground. "Reckon that's a rattler?"

"Nah. It's a rat snake. The skin was hanging from the rafters."

Jim looked skeptical. "Still could be a rattler."

"No, sir, rattlers don't climb. Betcha a nickel it's a rat snake. Good kind of snake to have. They clear out the vermin." Jim grunted and folded his arms across his chest. The two men stared, entranced by the pretty view. Lucas's brother, Matt, had a home amidst a grove of oaks less than a mile to the south, the roof visible in the patch of trees. To the north, he could make out the roof of Thomas' home, his other brother, about the same distance away.

The breeze stirred something inside him. Gratitude. Humility. His uncle had made him an offer he hardly could believe.

He shook his head in wonder of the possibility. "A man could make every one of his dreams come true in a place like this."

His uncle gave him a wry smile. "We haven't shook on it yet."

Lucas smiled. "I know, I know."

He turned to face the log cabin, two rooms separated by a dogtrot. A grove of live oak surrounded the home. A pecan tree grew by the well a few paces off the front porch. He strolled over to the nut tree and picked up a couple of pecans. He cracked them in his fist.

His uncle shuffled over. "Ernestine made some mighty fine pies from these here pecans."

"Don't I know it. Best pecan pies in the county."

"Right," Uncle Jim said quietly.

His uncle rarely spoke of his late wife. When she passed away ten years ago, he'd packed up his belongings, sold off the livestock and left the ranch behind. Since then, he'd lived with relatives here and there, never settling in one spot for long.

The ranch had sat quiet for the past ten years, uninhabited by men or cattle. All in all, it was in decent shape, given the neglect. Lucas shouldn't get ahead of himself, he knew that, but relished the idea of owning this place, with his brothers within walking distance.

"Why don't you show me the cabin?" Lucas patted him on the shoulder. "It's been years since I've been inside."

Side by side, but in no particular hurry, they walked back to the cabin. Lucas studied the land with an experienced eye. The barn needed a coat of paint, and maybe some work on the roof. The corral looked serviceable.

Jim pushed one of the doors open. The hinges screeched. Cobwebs hung across the doorway. Lucas swatted them away and the two men went inside. A fireplace took up one side of the cabin. Soot darkened the grate and chimney. A wood box with a sagging lid flanked the fireplace. Massive wooden beams spanned the ceiling. Lucas could tell the cabin roof was in good repair. It looked like it would continue to survive the sometimes-violent spring storms.

"What did you say your momma's name was again?" Lucas asked.

Jim took off his hat. "Clementine."

"So if I have a daughter, I need to call her Clementine?"

"That's right."

"And that's all I gotta do?"

"That's right. Ernestine and me always figured we'd have us a few kids and we'd name a girl child Clementine."

Lucas nodded. "Aunt Ernestine was partial to the name too?"

"Her momma's name was Clementine as well."

11

"I'll be," Lucas murmured.

Jim's eyes watered. He turned away and wandered to the window. "I got enough money to tide me over till I go to meet my reward. I'm gonna live in Galveston with my sister. I just want to leave the place in good hands."

"And for me to name my daughter Clementine?"

"Right. Clementine Bentley. I like the sound of it."

"How do you know I'm going to have a daughter?"

"I don't know you're gonna have a daughter. Heck, you don't even have a wife."

Lucas held up his pointer finger. "Yet."

"You got any prospects?"

Lucas shrugged and grinned. "I got plenty of prospects."

Jim rolled his eyes. "Sure, I imagine a fine-looking young buck like you has admirers, but you got one in mind that you want to marry?"

"I do. Just between you and me, I'm sweet on Faith and Gracie's little sister. I haven't proposed properly. That's probably why she's a little reluctant, but I aim to pay her a visit."

Jim squinted at him. "And go down on one knee?"

"Why sure. I'll do whatever I need to do. I might even tell her we need to have us a baby girl and call her Clementine. Once I explain all that, she'll change her tune."

"What if she doesn't?"

"I'll throw her over my shoulder and carry her back to Texas. Once she sees this fine ranch, she'll be as eager as I am."

"If you don't take it, I'll just sell it and give the money to Josh Bentley."

Lucas frowned. His cousin held about five thousand acres south of Magnolia. Josh always held himself apart from Lucas and his brothers.

"I heard Josh's getting married," Lucas said.

His uncle shook his head. "Not anytime soon. His father left the ranch in debt and the bank's talking about foreclosing. Josh's fancy debutante fiancée told him she didn't want to marry a pauper. She claimed she was far too pretty to waste her looks on a poor man. She told him that and turned around and married a judge in New Orleans."

Lucas shrugged. "Sorry to hear that. Especially about the debt. I always thought his family did pretty well."

"Josh has worked hard and paid off his father's debts, but he says he's never marrying. I suppose his heart was broke."

"So, he obviously won't ever have a little Clementine."

"That's right. You and your brothers, much to my surprise, have shown yourselves to be the marrying kind. Family men. I like that. What's more, Ernestine always favored you, Lucas."

Lucas felt a wave of warmth come over him, and surprise too. His aunt never acted like she favored him or anyone, truth be told. Aunt Ernestine was stern, and unfriendly, and tall... taller than her husband by several inches. She was pale, wore her hair pulled back in a severe knot that Lucas always wanted to loosen just a tad. He wondered if it might improve her disposition. The few memories he had of Aunt Ernestine were of her fussing at him for a variety of shortcomings. His face was grubby. His table manners atrocious. He cussed.

He didn't recall her showing much fondness, but it was hard to tell with some folks.

"I'd rather keep it in the Bentley family. I want you boys to have the land, but I want you to run things. I think you're the man to take this land and make it something special."

Lucas nodded, unsure what to say. "Thank you. I'm honored."

13

Jim grew teary-eyed once again as he crossed the room, his hand outstretched. "I'll give you two months. Get married in two months and I'll hand over the deed."

Lucas couldn't hide his excitement. He smiled as large as he ever had, reached out his hand and gave his uncle a firm handshake. "Done."

Chapter Three

Hope

Hope arrived at work as early as daylight allowed. A new box of books, the latest shipment from the small press in Philadelphia, sat on the counter. She still had ten minutes or so to look through the contents and then she'd have to open the shop. Usually, a few patrons would be outside the door each morning. To make them wait wouldn't do at all. Or that's what Mr. Jones always said.

She untied the cord and tugged off the lid to reveal the titles of the new books, hopeful to find a new favorite, or at least a new, popular book that would have customer's talking. But all the books were the same title, *Miss Millicent Visits the Cavalry*. An illustration of a buxom young woman adorned the cover. What on earth had Mr. Jones ordered? Tentatively, she opened the top book, read a few lines and yanked her hand back.

Slamming the lid back down, she gasped. "Oh, dear. Oh dear, oh dear."

A knock at the front door interrupted her work. Patrons had already queued up and waited to enter the shop. She shoved the box aside. Later, when the shop was closed, she'd write the company a letter. She'd politely request to return the books.

She hurried to the front of the shop, turned the sign around and unlocked the door. There was no line of people, just a single, familiar man. Cyrus Stearns leaned against the bench in front of the store. He gave her an oily grin. "Why, don't you look as pretty as can be. When are you going to let me take you out for a promenade? I'm tired of waiting."

Hope managed, barely, to hold back a shudder of disgust. Instead, she schooled her features into a cordial expression. She smiled, but with a hint of cool disdain.

"Hello, Cyrus, have you come to do some book shopping?"

"I've come to see the prettiest girl in Boston and think about what it would be like to kiss her."

The thought made her stomach churn. She shook her head and tried to find a response that would adequately express her disinterest. She often considered giving him a piece of her mind when he bothered her with ungentlemanly comments or offers, but she had to remember that he owned the building. If she offended him, he might cause Mr. Jones trouble.

He ambled over to the counter, and, with a quick movement, tossed the box lid to the side.

"They're not for sale," Hope blurted. She snatched the lid from the floor and tried desperately to slam it back onto the box. Cyrus, however, swatted the lid away, sending it clattering to the floor again.

"Why, Miss O'Brian," he drawled. His grin widened as he grabbed the first book. He flipped through the pages and sniggered. "What kind of books are you and Old Man Jones selling here?"

"The books were ordered on accident. I mean to send them back."

Cyrus waved the book in the air. "Not this one. This one is mine. Send me a bill. Come to think of it, I'll just take the whole box."

He tucked the box under his arm and strolled out of the bookshop, whistling all the while. Hope let out a groan of exasperation. Now what? Would Cyrus tell the world that Mr. Jones sold unsavory, untoward books?

Over the next few days, she waited. Mr. Jones came to work each day, slightly disheveled, and muttering under his breath, but never mentioned the books. He must have forgotten. By the end of the week, she almost dared to hope that he might have completely overlooked the mistaken order, but then another box arrived with more scandalous books. Instead of leaving them on the counter, she dragged them to the back of the store and tucked them away.

The next morning, when Mr. Jones shuffled into the store, his shirt misbuttoned, and his tie far too short, she took matters in hand.

"Sir, I've decided it's time I take charge of all ordering."

He knit his busy brows, stared at her for a long moment, and then brightened. "Mish O'Brian! So nice to see you. My, you've grown up." With that, he patted her on the head and shambled to the back offices.

She let out a sigh as she watched his retreating figure. Poor Mr. Jones. He wasn't the same man he'd been when she first started working for him.

"Something wrong with him?" Cyrus asked.

Hope drew a sharp breath. She hadn't heard Cyrus enter the shop, but there he was, standing in the doorway, his eyes big as plums as he watched Mr. Jones retreat to the back of the store.

"Of course not." The lie fell from her lips before she could stop it. It wasn't her fault, or so she told herself. It was simply an unthinking response, but when she didn't correct her words, she felt a deep sense of shame. Of course, she wanted to protect Mr. Jones, but she wasn't a person who lied.

Cyrus sneered. "I should give you the shop. You could do better than that old geezer, and then you'd be beholden to me. And I'd like that."

Hope's mouth went dry. Her throat tightened. To own her own bookshop sounded like a dream. She could read all day if she owned a bookshop, and Cyrus dangled the possibility right before her eyes. What an astonishing opportunity, but one that came at a terrible price. She could have her heart's desire, but she'd have to betray Mr. Jones.

"I don't want a bookshop," she said. Another lie. "Not at that price." That part was actually true.

Cyrus scowled and rolled his eyes. "The word in the neighborhood is that you're nothing but a cold fish. All the fellas around here say that you're never going to be anything other than a shop girl. An old maid. You ought to be a little friendlier."

He stormed out of the shop, slamming the door behind him.

"Good riddance," Hope muttered. She wondered what he meant by 'word in the neighborhood'. Was Cyrus friends with the man who followed her home? The man who tried to engage her in conversation. She wandered to the window and gazed out onto the street, a shiver running up her spine.

Chapter Four

Lucas

Four days in a cramped sleeping compartment on a train made him feel a mite surly. What with the jostling and rattling, he'd barely slept a wink. At least, once he arrived in Boston, he'd gotten a hotel room with a proper bed, one he could stretch out in. Another good thing about the hotel was its location. It was directly across from the bookshop where Hope worked.

Handy.

After breakfast, he strolled across the street. In his pocket, he had a piece of paper with an agreement, terms written out for her. Fortunately for him, his sisters-in-law were more than happy to help him make a list of all the things that would entice Hope to marry him.

For one, he'd have to agree to bring her personal library, which was vast, to Texas.

He left out the part about the cabin, the new ranch, and that if God ever blessed them with a daughter, they'd have to call her Clementine. He hadn't shared that detail with Faith or Grace either. He figured there would be plenty of time for that once he got back to Texas with his reluctant bride. Besides, she might not even want a family. She might simply want to play the part of his wife.

Which was fine. He'd still end up with his ranch.

If she didn't agree, Lucas wouldn't have time to court another woman. Uncle Jimmy would sell the ranch out from under him despite all the improvements Lucas had made in the last month. He'd give the money to Josh and that irked Lucas to no end.

No, he'd have to do his best to convince Hope O'Brian.

Lucas stared at the bookshop door for a long moment, trying to imagine how a conversation with the girl might go. He grimaced, let out a deep sigh, gripped the doorknob and turned. The bell rang as he pushed through the door of the bookshop. Hope stood behind the counter, her gaze fixed on the book she held. She was redheaded, of course. Shorter than Grace or Faith, and while his two sisters-in-law were slim, Hope was decidedly not. Her figure was curvy, very feminine. The sight of her made him stop and stare like a fool.

Engrossed in her book, she hardly noticed him. "Good morning," she murmured and flipped the page.

"Mornin'."

"Could I help you find something?" She spoke without lifting her gaze.

His mouth was dry. His chest felt tight, probably some discomfort from sleeping on the train. That's what he told himself as he stood, rooted to the spot. "No, ma'am."

She lifted her gaze and studied him with the prettiest, bluest eyes he'd ever seen. She blinked, her pale skin blushed with a hint of pink. For some reason he couldn't fathom, she frowned at him and dropped her gaze back to her book, forcibly ignoring him. He wondered what he'd done to earn her displeasure. He hadn't said much. Usually, whenever he caused a fancy lady some offense, it came after a little conversation. Some ladies just didn't care for his direct manner.

20

He rubbed his jaw, pondering his situation. Should he just lay the agreement out for her while the shop was empty? Wait till he'd had a moment to collect his thoughts? He hadn't imagined having such a strong reaction to the stubborn girl. Thoughts buzzed in his mind, like a hive of bewildered bees.

When he arrived in Boston the prior evening, he'd booked his return ticket, paying for a sleeper car that would accommodate his wife and him. That train would leave in two days, plenty of time to make his offer to Hope, and marry her too. Or so he assumed. Which meant he should march up to the counter, hand her the agreement and propose.

The clock was ticking, in more ways than one. After all, she was well on her way to becoming a spinster, one who lived her life with her nose in a book. He'd mentioned that a time or two in his list. Surely, she'd welcome his plan. Not that he was any great catch, just a handsome, charming cowboy, one that could offer her a life of adventure. What he imagined would interest her was the notion of seeing her sisters, and the babies they expected.

"Sir," a stern voice came from behind him. "You're in the way."

"Pardon me," he said absentmindedly and ambled to the back of the bookshop. There, he made a show of examining the shelves, selecting various volumes and leafing through the pages, all the while keeping his gaze fixed on the girl.

He couldn't help himself. She was lovely.

Far prettier than he imagined. He'd always thought Grace and Faith were pretty, but their younger sister had a beauty that was all her own. A single tendril had escaped her coifed hair. Every so often she'd twirl it between her fingers as she read her book.

People came and went. She greeted them with a smile and friendly word, but if they didn't need help, she went right back to her book. Her inattention made a slow burn of irritation heat his blood. Was she always so distracted? He growled, and a nearby shopper, an elderly woman, gaped at him and edged away.

A young man set some books on the counter and took out his wallet. Only then did she set her novel aside and wait on her customer.

He recalled what Faith and Grace had told him about Hope. *When our sister isn't reading, she's daydreaming. Or gathering wool.*

He'd take her home to Texas and she could do her woolgathering and help him claim a thousand acres of prime grazing. While she daydreamed, she'd be under his roof, near him, a notion that pleased him more with each passing moment.

People came and left the store, some buying books, others merely perusing the shelves. He waited impatiently. Over the next hour, the shop grew steadily quieter, until he was the only customer. He knew he should talk to her now, before anyone else came in.

Shifting his weight from foot to foot, he patted his pocket. The paper crinkled under his palm, reassuring him somewhat, but not quite enough to go ahead with his plan. Hope was petite. He was probably close to twice her size and he might startle her. He knew Grace and Faith were a little skittish, or had been when they first came to Magnolia. Thomas had mentioned that their father was a rough type of fellow, one who'd scared his wife and daughters. Lucas wondered if he might frighten a girl like Hope.

As he pondered the finer points of his dilemma, the doorbell rang.

"Aw, heck," he muttered.

A lady entered the shop, an elegant, older woman. She seemed to be an acquaintance, one that Hope greeted by name, a Mrs. Caldicott. Lucas recalled Faith talking about Mrs. Caldicott. The woman offered Hope a gift, a box of sweets, and they chatted about the book that Hope had been reading.

When Mrs. Caldicott asked about news from Magnolia, Lucas listened intently.

"I got a letter just yesterday," Hope said. "Faith says she and Thomas are expecting."

Mrs. Caldicott pressed her hand to her heart. "Oh, my. I can hardly believe it. I know it's selfish of me, but I'd half-hoped she wouldn't like Texas and she'd return to civilization to once more be my companion. I miss her so."

"I do as well," Hope said. "The only time I don't miss my sisters is when I can escape into a book."

"No thoughts on visiting?"

Lucas couldn't hold back a grin.

"If I go, I'll be outnumbered."

"What do you mean?"

"Two against one. Grace and Faith will give me no end of grief if I don't agree to stay and marry that detestable Lucas Bentley."

Lucas scoffed. Detestable? He'd been called a few things in his life, but detestable was a new one.

"Is someone here?" Mrs. Caldicott asked.

"No, I don't believe so."

"I thought I just heard someone cough."

"Nobody's here. I had several customers earlier, but they've all left. I'm alone. Anyway, I've decided that I'll go visit them as soon as the beastly brother-in-law is married."

Lucas shook his head and rubbed the back of his neck.

"You're not worried he might pay you a visit and entice you back to Texas, as he promised?"

"He didn't promise to 'entice me'. He promised far more primitive means, tossing me over his shoulder and whatnot." She snickered. "He might change his mind if he knew how many bonbons I've been eating lately."

She patted her hip to emphasize her point.

Lucas snorted. Hope was perfect in his eyes.

Mrs. Caldicott shook her head. "You're Rubenesque. And the picture of loveliness. Lucas Bentley would be a very lucky man if you were to accept his proposal of marriage."

"I don't think I belong there."

"Where do you belong?" Mrs. Caldicott asked.

"With me," Lucas said softly, to himself.

"Boston is so lonely without my sisters. I miss them more every day." Hope sighed. "I just don't know where I belong anymore."

"But I do," he said under his breath. "I know right where you belong."

Chapter Five

Hope

When it was time for Mrs. Caldicott to leave, Hope saw her to the door and thanked her for stopping by and for the thoughtful gift. Hope remained at the door and watched her until she disappeared. Someone behind her coughed softly. She whirled around.

A man stood a few paces away. Tall, dark-haired, he wore a bemused smile. She gasped.

"Sorry," he said, his tone friendly. "I hoped I wouldn't startle you."

She swallowed hard and tried to compose herself. "It's f-fine."

"Could I get your help with a book?"

"Yes, of course."

"It's something for my nephew."

Hope tried to calm her quaking heart. The man looked like he'd stepped out of a novel in the children's section. A story about swashbuckling pirates, terribly handsome in a roguish way and, judging from his swagger, probably knew he was fine-looking.

She helped him select several books, but when she discovered the boy was only eleven, she offered a few other suggestions, more right for a boy. His manner of speaking made her wonder where he was from. He didn't have the clipped speech of a Boston native, more of a southern drawl.

He was exceedingly polite, answering her questions with a *yes, ma'am* or *no, ma'am*. But when they returned to the counter, a customer entered the shop, a young man who stopped by once a week to buy a novel for his ailing mother. Hope was about to greet him, but the tall stranger spoke first.

"Would you mind coming back a little later, son?"

"Well... I j-just wanted to get a book." The young man reddened as he stammered.

"I understand. I promise they'll still be here later, or better yet, tomorrow." The stranger moved towards the entry, prompting the young man to scramble out the door.

Hope stared in astonishment as the stranger locked the door. Backing away from him, she tried to gain some distance. The wall behind her stopped her retreat. She let out a whimper when she banged against it. "Are you friends with the man who follows me at night?"

His eyes darkened. "Someone's following you? At night?"

He banged his fist on the counter and gritted his teeth. Coins in the money drawer jangled. He peered under the counter. Hope followed his gaze to the drawer where receipts and money were kept. The man wasn't her pursuer, clearly, but he eyed the money with what seemed more than just idle curiosity. Another fearsome possibility came to her. He intended to rob her. Mercy, she'd heard of other shops getting robbed in broad daylight, but never imagined such a thing could happen in her bookshop.

"There's very little money," she whispered, edging away. "Very little."

"Beg your pardon?"

"You can take it, just take it."

His jaw slackened, dropping a fraction of an inch. Then he laughed, a deep reverberating sound that filled the shop. "Sweetheart, I'm not here to rob you. I'm Lucas Bentley. I came to Boston to propose to you. Told you I'd do that if need be. The need became pretty clear when you quit writing me."

"What?" she breathed. The situation dawned on her slowly. She clapped her hand over her mouth to keep from screaming. Despite her efforts, a small whimper escaped her lips. She shook her head. Her face heated, burning with shock and dismay.

"No," she whispered. "I've had nightmares that start just like this. Lucas Bentley surprising me in some horrifying way. Tell me I'm dreaming."

Lucas shrugged. "All right. You're dreaming."

He reached inside his pocket. She yelped. The sound had come so suddenly, she hadn't been able to stifle it. She'd made the noise because she couldn't imagine what he intended.

With a weary sigh, he set a small piece of paper beside the stack of books they'd selected. "I know you probably wanted to meet me before agreeing to anything. That's why I came. I have a list of reasons why you oughta come to Texas."

She dropped her gaze to the paper.

"First off, you're going to want to be near your sisters, especially when they have a few young'uns running around. Second of all, Texas is warmer, and generally nicer. Just my opinion, but once you get to Magnolia, you'll see for yourself."

He went down the list, counting the reasons why she needed to come back with him. He mentioned things like her sisters missing her, she'd be a spinster soonish, she could open a bookstore in Magnolia if she wanted.

"I'd let you do that. Might be nice for you."

Lucas Bentley was a madman. She was certain. Faith and Grace had hinted at his eccentric personality, his being a little set in his ways, but it was so much more than that. He was a lunatic.

"Get out," she whispered.

"All right, Hope. I understand this might be a little overwhelming. Why, you're as pale as the driven snow. Which is another point I'd like to make. We won't have a bunch of snow and ice for you to contend with."

She folded her arms across her chest, hugging herself. "Would you kindly leave, Mr. Bentley?"

He grinned and lowered his voice, speaking in a conspiratorial tone. "I like the way you say my name."

His tone was sultry, teasing, and entirely inappropriate. Despite her ire, she shivered. He noticed. His grin widened.

"Please leave, Mr... erm... sir."

He scratched his jaw. "You bet. I'll come by tomorrow. We'll talk more then. I'll get my books. The train leaves the day after tomorrow, by the way."

"I won't be on that train," she said from between gritted teeth.

He waved off her words. "You'll come around. I'm prepared to do what I need to do to convince you. You know why?"

She held her breath.

"Because," he said. "I like you a lot better than I thought I would."

With a flirtatious wink, he turned and went to the door. He tried to turn the handle, but found the door locked. He jiggled the handle a little, grumbling under his breath. After a moment, he chuckled, unlatched the lock and let himself out, shutting the door firmly behind him.

Chapter Six

Lucas

The food at his hotel was good, fancy stuff, the likes of which he'd never tasted before. The kitchen boy, Paul, a young man of thirteen or fourteen, served him dish after dish. First, he brought a clear broth that he called consommé, followed by a salad, beef tenderloin with mushrooms and finally a slice of cake, which the boy referred to as Charlotte Russe.

"This looks pretty fussy," Lucas told him. "I'm not used to eating this sort of grub."

Paul grinned. "You eat cowboy food in Texas?"

Lucas gave him an answering smile. "All the time, fried rattlesnake mostly."

The boy's eyes widened. "Really?"

Lucas shook his head. "I'm kidding. I've never eaten rattlesnake, but I've heard some folks eat 'em. I'd have to be pretty hungry to have a rattler for dinner."

The boy chuckled and excused himself to go back to the kitchen. Lucas sat by the window. He'd requested the table, so he could watch Hope lock up and go home. He watched her hurry along the road, looking fretful, maybe because of their little talk. He hadn't intended to frighten her, and hoped she'd feel a little better tomorrow.

He had a powerful urge to go after her, to make sure she got home safely. It bothered him mightily that someone had followed her and frightened her. He'd seen a rough sort of fella peering in the windows of the bookshop that afternoon and had run him off. There weren't any more rough types now, but he still worried that some no-good ruffian might give her trouble.

Lucas imagined if they walked together, he might be able to try to impress her with his gallantry. He wasn't used to talking with the fairer sex. He spent more time in the saddle, alone and riding the range, than he did talking to people, never mind pretty young ladies.

A short while later, Paul returned. "Would you care for another piece, sir?"

"It's mighty tasty, but I'm full as a bedbug. I need to get back to Texas, so I can get away from this living high on the hog."

A movement outside caught his attention. In the last rays of dusk, an old man shuffled to the front door of the bookshop. He twisted the door handle, but found it locked. The sight of the old man trying to open the door reminded Lucas of his own fumbling with the shop's doorknob earlier that afternoon. He chided himself for his clumsiness. More than anything he wished he could have had a second chance with the reserved but stubborn O'Brian girl.

He'd come to Boston thinking he'd simply offer for her and she'd welcome his proposition. Never had he imagined a girl like Hope. The moment their eyes met, he felt as though he'd been kicked in the head by a mule. His thoughts had scattered until he'd corralled them into a single purpose: to woo and win the youngest O'Brian sister.

She'd thought he'd come to rob the bookshop, he recalled with a twist of embarrassment. She thought he was no more than a thug. He leaned back in his chair and studied the old

30

man, struggling to open the door. She'd regarded him as a threat, but now someone in fact looked as if he might want to break down the door and do some mischief. Not much mischief, judging from the man's frail stature.

"Who is that?"

"That's Mr. Jones. He owns the bookshop." Paul cleared the dessert plate and Lucas's coffee cup. "He used to come in here to eat lunch every day. Very nice man, but now he's a bit mixed up."

"That's a shame," Lucas murmured, wondering if that might work against him. Hope wouldn't want to leave the bookshop if she needed to help the ailing man. She might be as stubborn as the day was long, but she was a caring person. Faith and Grace went on about their little sister's kind heart.

"I thought for a minute he was up to no good," Lucas said.

"No, sir, he lives in an apartment over the bookshop."

The boy lingered at the table. Like Lucas, he watched Mr. Jones struggle to open the door. The elderly man shook his head and slowly grew more frustrated, trying the same key over and over, to no avail. People walked past him on the sidewalk, a few glanced at the man, but no one stopped to offer help. Lucas wondered if that was how things were done here in Boston. Nobody took the time to help a person with troubles.

Lucas growled softly. "Let me pay you. Then I'll go see if I can help him. Sun's going down. It's getting cold."

"I can put it on your account, sir. Look... he's got it."

Mr. Jones had, at last, managed to open his door. Lucas watched as the weary gentleman staggered inside and shut the door behind himself.

"All right, then," Lucas said, rising from his chair. "Thank you, son. That was a fine meal."

"Sorry it wasn't rattlesnake, Mr. Bentley."

Lucas chuckled and returned to his room on the third floor. From his window, he could see directly into the bookshop as well as into Mr. Jones's apartment. Lamplight flickered, but he couldn't see the man. He was being a busybody, he decided, and turned away from the window.

He rubbed the back of his neck, groaning. How could doing practically nothing all day make a man tired as a dog and his muscles stiff and sore? He yearned to finish up his business in Boston as soon as he could... make Hope his, arrange for her books to be sent, then get on the train and go home to Texas. He'd need to choose his words wisely, try to show Hope that they'd get along well. He paced the room, trying to think of pretty words.

"Hope, I reckon you're as pretty as a flower. Even prettier."

That sounded all right, but what if she asked what kind of flower? Maybe a bluebonnet. No, that wouldn't do. Not at all. Grace had told him and his brothers they didn't have bluebonnets in Boston.

"You smell like freshly cut hay."

That sounded all right, and if she asked what kind of hay, he would have a world of names to offer.

"I promise to care for you and protect you from all harm."

He smiled, congratulating himself on his progress. He needed more words just like that, and to forget about his list. He wished he hadn't left the list with her. She might take offense at his suggestion she was a spinster. Tomorrow, bright and early, he'd march right into the bookstore and apologize to her for the whole disastrous first meeting.

With a glimmer of renewed confidence, he returned to the window, brushing the lace curtain aside. He stared, hardly believing what he saw. Flames shot from the roof of the bookshop. Smoke billowed from a broken window and fire licked the eaves.

The street below was empty. His first thought was of Hope. He prayed she hadn't returned to the bookshop. He recalled the elderly gentleman, struggling to get inside the shop and felt certain he was still in the building. Lucas raced out of his room and down the stairs, nearly knocking over several hotel guests in his haste.

Chapter Seven

Hope

Hope awoke just before dawn, her first thought as she opened her eyes was of Lucas Bentley, and his appearance in the bookshop the prior day. Never in her life had she been so astonished. Dressing by the light of her lamp, she imagined what she would tell him if he returned. Or when he returned. From what she knew of the Bentley brothers, they were tenacious. A tingle of apprehension made her shiver.

As the youngest of the O'Brian sisters, she had few memories of her parents. She had enough to remember some of her father's terrible outbursts. She recalled hiding under the bed with Grace and Faith while he raged.

She didn't think Lucas had a temper. He seemed lighthearted and she sensed a kindness in him. Yesterday he'd tried his best to be charming here and there. And yet how could one ever really know about a man's true nature until it was tested?

He promised that he'd do anything to convince her to go to Texas. What did that mean? He smiled while he said the words, but she found the sentiment somewhat threatening. She finished dressing and was about to put on her boots when she recalled a letter that he'd written some months past. She rummaged through the drawers of her bedside table. In her haste, she bumped the table. A stack of books piled on the table tumbled to the floor.

She had letters from Faith and Grace, plenty of them, but where were the letters from Lucas? Then she found them tucked inside an Austen novel, tied with a crimson ribbon. When had she done that? Perhaps it was when she'd written him to say she wouldn't come.

The paper crinkled as she opened one of the letters. A sudden rush of warmth came over her. Running her fingers over the writing, she imagined him sitting down to pen a letter to her. There was nothing subtle about Lucas Bentley. He wrote in a bold and direct manner and this time when she read the words, something between the lines and the words themselves, endeared him to her.

She shook her head, trying to clear her thoughts, reminding herself of his forceful manner. He was arrogant. Impossible. Yesterday, he'd suggested his offer would save her from a pitiful life as a spinster. Tossing the letter aside, she let out a huff of indignation.

With some difficulty, she composed herself and went downstairs to the kitchen. The servants had laid out a light breakfast of tea, milk, sweet rolls and bacon. Usually, she was the first one down, but this morning two of the boarders sat at the table, talking excitedly. She bid them good morning and poured herself a cup of tea.

"Mrs. Spencer threw her out on her ear, she did," said the older girl.

"No! In the middle of the night?"

"Near enough. She said she wouldn't put up with slatternly behavior and unladylike deportment."

"Bless her. She'll be hard-pressed to find a boarding house that will take her in after that. Mrs. Spencer won't give her a reference, that's for certain."

Hope would have liked to linger to hear more. She told herself that she didn't have time for idle chatter, however, and wrapped two sweet rolls in a linen napkin. One of them she'd give to Mr. Jones, since the servants always made plenty.

Her walk to the bookshop took a little longer than usual. The streets were especially busy. A light mist fell, making her shiver. Preoccupied with thoughts of Lucas and what she would say when she saw him, she hardly noticed the cold. By the time she turned down the street toward the bookshop, she had her response mostly worked out. Instead of refusing Lucas, she'd tell him she needed more time. A delay would be the perfect answer. It was neither a yes nor a no and might satisfy him and, more importantly, send him on his way.

A crowd gathered in the street. Hope hurried to see what the people stared at. As she drew near, she took in the sight of the bookshop. "Heavens," she whispered.

A pile of smoldering embers lay where the bookshop had once stood.

Chapter Eight

Lucas

No one in the crowd noticed Hope, but Lucas did. He saw her turn down the street, her brow knit as she walked, deep in thought. He saw her eyes widen with disbelief, then distress, as she drew near. He pushed his way through the mob, trying to reach her. And when he got close, he saw her sway on her feet, struggling to stay standing despite the people jostling her from all sides.

He caught her as she fainted.

Hemmed in by the mass of people, his temper flared. "Make way," he snarled. "Or I'll start cracking heads."

A ridiculous threat. With an unconscious woman in his arms, he could hardly carry out his promise. His threat worked well enough, though, perhaps because he stood half a head taller than most of the other men in the crowd. They moved back. He was able to carry Hope to the entrance of the hotel.

He took her to the parlor, where he laid her gently on a chaise. A few guests gave him curious looks, but after the events of the prior night, no one seemed overly surprised that a young woman had fainted.

Paul came from the kitchen with a pot of tea. "I saw you coming, sir."

"Thank you. Bring me a blanket."

A moment later, the boy returned with a wool blanket and Lucas draped it across her.

She whimpered. Her lids fluttered. She opened her eyes and gave a cry of dismay. "Lucas Bentley!"

He sat on the chair beside her. "At your service."

She looked aghast and he wanted to point out that he'd just plucked her from the middle of a mob after she'd fainted. He let it go. She could thank him later.

"She's the girl who works at the bookshop," Paul said.

Hope looked around in confusion. "Where am I?"

"The hotel across from the bookshop."

"The Hotel Elizabeth?"

"That's right," Lucas said. "I'm staying here."

"The bookshop," she whispered. "Mr. Jones!"

"The shop burned down," Paul said. "Last night. Mr. Jones is safe. You'll never believe who rescued him."

"The fire brigade?" she said, struggling to sit up.

"No, Miss, not the fire brigade. They got into a brawl while the building burned down."

"The important thing," Lucas said, "is that Mr. Jones is unharmed. His sister took him to her home. He's resting there."

A woman appeared in the doorway of the parlor. Lucas recognized her from the bookstore yesterday. Mrs. Caldicott, looking horror-stricken, cried out with dismay as she rushed into the room. She looked a fair bit different than she did yesterday, not near as elegant. She'd probably hurried over. Lucas imagined he probably didn't look too swell himself.

He stood and gave her a respectful nod.

Mrs. Caldicott and Hope embraced.

"I came as soon as I heard, my dear Hope," Mrs. Caldicott said tearfully.

"It's too awful to bear," Hope spoke, her voice choked with emotion. "There's nothing left. The firemen fought in the street while the books burned."

Mrs. Caldicott sank onto the chaise beside Hope. "Beastly men. They fight to be the one to put out the fire, so they can collect the insurance money. Meanwhile the fire takes everything." She turned to Lucas. "Who are you, sir?"

"Lucas Bentley, ma'am."

She didn't respond right away. Instead, she stared at him, a bewildered expression on her face. After a long moment, she spoke slowly. "Pleased to meet you. I'm Lucille Caldicott."

"I've heard about you," he said.

"Likewise, Mr. Bentley."

Mrs. Caldicott and Hope spoke for a few minutes more until Mrs. Caldicott insisted on taking Hope to her home to rest. Hope had suffered a dreadful shock and Mrs. Caldicott wanted to tend to her in her own home. Lucas would have liked to tend to Hope himself, but he could see there was no arguing.

"Just for a short while," the woman said when she noted his exasperation.

He helped her to Mrs. Caldicott's carriage and watched with a sinking heart as the women left. He growled in frustration. Last night had been a trial. Despite his efforts to work with the small bucket brigade, the shop had burned to the ground. The firemen hadn't approved of the neighbors trying to control the fire and Lucas had scuffled with a few of them.

"I'm starting to dislike Boston," he muttered.

Up in his room, he took a bath, trying to get rid of the smoky smell and grit. He dressed in clean clothes and had lunch. As the day wore on, he grew more and more restless.

Finally, he decided to pay a visit to the boarding house. That would be the best bet since there was no reason for Hope to return to the bookshop.

He walked and arrived in the late afternoon. A girl sat at the desk and greeted him with a smile. "Why, hello there."

Lucas felt his face warm. "Afternoon. Are you Mrs. Spencer?"

"No," she giggled. "I'm Felicity. I'm new here."

"I'd like to speak to Miss O'Brian, please."

Her smile faded. "She's not here. If you like, you can wait in her room. Second floor, first door on the right."

"That doesn't sound very gentlemanly," Lucas said. "To wait in a young lady's room."

She gave him a coy look. "I won't tell if you don't. Besides, the landlady will run you off if she sees you in the parlor."

Despite her words, Lucas felt certain waiting in her room was untoward, but he also knew he had very little time left to make his case to Hope. He thanked the girl and trudged upstairs. With each step, he grew more convinced that waiting for Hope in her room wasn't the way to go about things, but he was running out of choices. All was fair in love and war, wasn't that what they said?

He let himself into her room and sighed happily. It was something special to step into Hope's world. Her scent hung in the air. He was intruding, in an awful way, he knew that. But the notion didn't trouble him. He ran his palm over the quilt on her bed, imagining her sleeping here. She was small and vulnerable. The girl downstairs had just let him, a stranger, walk right into Hope's room.

The oversight made him more determined than ever to make Hope his. He'd keep a watchful eye on the youngest O'Brian. Living in Texas, as his wife, she'd gain a measure of protection. God willing, with time, they'd grow close and perhaps even have a family.

With a chuckle, he lay back, resting his head on her pillow. He hadn't slept a wink last night on account of the fire. It was about five in the morning when all was said and done. Despite his exhaustion, he hadn't let himself rest. He'd needed to wait for Hope. He knew the fire would come as a terrible shock and vowed to help her in her moment of distress. It had been a long, grueling night and now a wave of fatigue came over him. He sank deeper into the blankets and closed his eyes.

Chapter Nine

Hope

Seated in the elegant carriage, Hope rode to Mrs. Caldicott's home, trying to compose herself. In her mind, she pictured Lucas's face as she'd left. He looked displeased and disheartened. To her surprise, parting from him made her feel a little bereft. How could that be, she wondered.

They settled in Mrs. Caldicott's parlor, sitting near the fire that crackled in the grate. Mrs. Caldicott, always the picture of stylishness and decorum, looked a sight. To Hope's astonishment, Mrs. Caldicott had left the house not only without gloves but with her hair unbound. The woman's hands shook as she handed Hope a cup of tea. The tea sloshed precariously.

"I can't begin to tell you how frightened I was to hear of the bookshop," she said.

"It's a tragedy, to be sure. Mr. Jones's father started the bookstore seventy-five years ago. It was in a different location, but still, I'm not sure what Mr. Jones will do now. I'm not sure what I'll do either."

Poor Mr. Jones. Over the last few months, for some reason, he'd appeared more and more befuddled. She couldn't imagine his terror when the fire started and burned through the bookshop. A pang of grief squeezed her heart. All those books, hundreds and hundreds of books, were gone now. She sipped her tea, reminding herself the important thing was that Mr. Jones was safe.

Mrs. Caldicott offered her a plate of cookies, but Hope declined.

"What about this Mr. Bentley?" Mrs. Caldicott asked. "Has he come to court you?"

"I suppose he has. His sudden appearance is quite shocking. He gave me no warning that he'd come to Boston to seek me out."

"Other than to threaten to come and carry you off."

Mrs. Caldicott's tone was gently mocking. At times, the woman seemed to find the Bentley brothers a source of amusement.

Hope laughed softly. "I never expected him to make good on his threat! What sort of man says that sort of thing to a woman? In fact, he was in the shop yesterday when you came to visit."

Mrs. Caldicott's jaw dropped. "No!"

"He heard me call him a beastly brother-in-law. He said he was prepared to do whatever it required to win my hand."

"Oh," Mrs. Caldicott murmured. Her eyes got a faraway look in them. "He said he wants to win your hand. That puts a different light on things. It's quite romantic. Gallant, you might say."

"I'm not certain what his precise words were, but I do think he's unbalanced. He had a list of reasons I should marry him. He said he was going to save me from being an old maid... or maybe it was an old spinster. I don't recall." She set her tea aside and rubbed her temples. "The last day has been more than I can bear."

Mrs. Caldicott's lips still tugged up into a soft smile. "Do you have any feelings for him?"

"Feelings? Yes, of course I do. Intense dislike."

Mrs. Caldicott kept her appraising look fixed on her and she felt her skin warm under her scrutiny.

"Well..." Hope bit her lip. "He came for me when I was in the crowd. I fainted. He caught me..."

"Go on."

"As I came to, I was sorry he wasn't still holding me." Hope put her palm to her cheek to try and cool the burn of embarrassment.

Mrs. Caldicott's brows lifted. "I see."

Hope swallowed hard, trying to tamp down her awkwardness. "And when he calls me sweetheart, he makes my heart melt a little. But then I fretted, what if Lucas Bentley started the fire?"

"Merciful heavens, what a ghastly thought!"

"It is. I can't imagine asking him."

A knock at the door drew her attention. One of Mrs. Caldicott's servants waited, looking bashful. "Begging your pardon, Miss O'Brian. I didn't mean to overhear."

"What is it, Annabelle?"

"My brother works in the fire brigade. He said that the gentleman in the bookshop was rescued by a fellow by the name of Lucas Bentley. He charged into the burning building, ran to the top of the house and carried Mr. Jones out. My brother told me Mr. Jones set the fire himself when he knocked over a lamp."

Mrs. Caldicott smiled. "Well, that certainly speaks well of Mr. Bentley, doesn't it?"

Annabelle blushed. "I think your Mr. Bentley is a hero, if you don't mind my saying."

Hope was too astonished to reply. Her sisters had written letters praising Lucas, but she'd discounted their words. She'd assumed they simply wanted to entice her to the wild and woolly lands of Texas.

Mrs. Caldicott ordered lunch for them, insisting that she stay and eat before returning home. Hope tried her best to show her appreciation for her efforts, but her appetite had vanished. She managed a little soup but declined the poached chicken and dessert.

"I'm sorry," she said quietly. "I don't quite feel myself."

Mrs. Caldicott patted her hand. "Of course, dear. I'll have Phipps order the carriage and I'll accompany you."

"I hate to be so much trouble."

"It's no trouble at all. I must see you home myself. I won't take no for an answer."

Chapter Ten

Lucas

He was pretty clear that resting in a woman's bed was a poor idea, particularly if she hadn't exactly given her permission. He'd never been one on asking for permission, however. Still, he hadn't expected to wake up with someone's hands around his neck, squeezing the life out of him.

"What are ya doin' in Miss O'Brian's bed? Filthy cur!"

Lucas coughed and gagged.

"Answer me! She'd never take up with a fella. Not Miss O'Brian."

In the dim shadows, Lucas made out a man's face, older and grizzled. The man clutched his throat with one hand and waved gardening shears in the other. Lucas swatted the man's hand from his throat. He didn't care to resort to violence, but he didn't like the sharp blades getting so close to his face either. When the man refused to release his grip, Lucas shoved him.

The man flew back, staggered a few steps, but lunged towards Lucas to renew his attack. Lucas snarled and lurched to his feet. Straightening to his full height seemed to slow his assailant. The man's eyes widened. The reprieve, however, didn't last long. The man came at him again with renewed fury.

Lucas side-stepped the man easily enough. He turned and, with a push, sent the man sprawling onto Hope's bed. With a deft motion, he pinned the man. The fellow was furious but didn't weigh more than a young calf and Lucas had plenty of practice wrestling those ornery critters.

"Don't hurt him," a woman shouted from behind him.

Lucas glanced over his shoulder as he kept a firm grip on the shear-wielding intruder. A woman stood in the doorway, pale and shaking. Her gray hair was swept into a tight arrangement, giving her a severe look. Lucas studied her while the man thrashed and cursed.

"Are you Mrs. Spencer?"

The woman gasped. "I am. And that is my gardener you're assaulting."

"Your gardener was about to give me a close shave with his pruning shears."

"What on earth are you doing in Miss O'Brian's room?"

The gardener continued to flail and curse a blue streak. Lucas glared at him. "Quit that cussing. There's a lady in the room."

"What on earth?" A soft voice came from the corridor. Hope appeared in the doorway. "Lucas," she murmured. "No, no, no."

"Would you tell this fella that I didn't hurt you?" Lucas released the man, half-expecting him to go on the attack once again. He didn't, thankfully. Instead, he heaved himself from the bed, wincing and trying to straighten his rumpled shirt.

"You know this man?" Mrs. Spencer demanded.

"Yes," Hope said tentatively. "I do."

Mrs. Spencer gave a huff of outrage. Her face reddened as she glowered at Hope and then Lucas and then back to Hope.

Her mouth opened and closed, like a gaffed trout as she struggled for something to say.

"I came to propose," Lucas said. "The gal downstairs said I should wait here. I was up all night trying to put out a fire since you people can't seem to agree who gets to throw water on a burning building. I came in here, and figured I'd get a little shut eye. Your gardener woke me up. Rudely, I might add."

Hope sank against the doorframe, looking downcast. He might have had a little sympathy for her if he hadn't started feeling a mite irritated with the entire town of Boston. He didn't care for their hospitality one bit.

Mrs. Spencer dismissed him with a wave of her hand and turned to face Hope. "I don't know if you intend to accept this young man's proposal. My advice is to refuse him. He's uncouth. A ruffian and no gentleman. I'll also recommend you seek new accommodations. Immediately. You know my rules, and you know I never bend them. Gabriel, please see the young man out."

Lucas snorted. "Him and who else? I'm not leaving without Hope."

Scowling, Mrs. Spencer swept out of the room.

The gardener shook his head and spoke gently. "Don't worry, lass, the wife and me will come up with something."

Hope's eyes filled with tears. Lucas, moved by her response, went to her, taking her hand in his. "My train leaves in the morning. Come with me. I have a place for us, high atop a hill. From the front porch you can see both Faith's and Grace's homes."

She looked up at him. Tears spilled from her eyes and rolled down her cheeks.

He lifted his hand and softly wiped them away. Her cheek felt silken beneath his work-roughened hands. Warmth traveled the length of his arm and gathered in his chest. He spoke softly, "Don't cry, sweetheart."

Chapter Eleven

Hope

Hope O'Brian might have been able to resist Lucas. There was a real chance she could have said no, right up till the moment he called her sweetheart. In that instant, her defenses crumbled. Her answer, a softly whispered *yes*, fell from her lips. And with that she agreed. But Gabriel interceded immediately, threatening Lucas with not-so-vague promises of bodily harm if he set out for Texas, with Hope, unmarried.

Gabriel instructed Lucas that he should not leave the boarding house. Then he went to find a minister to marry them, and to notify Hope's closest friends that they needed to come, now. Mrs. Caldicott was sent for and Mr. Jones as well. The bookshop owner sent his regrets, saying his sister insisted he remain in her home to recover from the effects of the fire.

Thirty minutes later, Lucas and Hope said their vows amid Mrs. Spencer's beautiful rose gardens. At first, Mrs. Spencer refused to allow the marriage, saying Lucas was unfit to marry any woman, Hope especially, but she changed her mind when Lucas offered to pay for the privilege. They were married beneath Gabriel's prized rose bower. When the vows were complete, Lucas brushed a soft kiss across her lips.

The rest of the day and the next morning were a blur of activity. Mrs. Spencer grudgingly agreed to allow Hope to spend one more night. This gave her a chance to pack her clothes and books and the rest of her belongings.

Gabriel brought her four large, slightly battered trunks that had belonged to his father. Lucas offered to pay Gabriel for the trunks, but Gabriel refused, saying Hope was like a daughter to him, and this way the trunks would remain in the family.

She kissed Gabriel on the cheek and bid him and his wife a heartfelt goodbye. Mrs. Caldicott came to the boarding house to see her off, giving Lucas stern instructions to take good care of her last O'Brian sister. She blinked back tears and waved goodbye as Hope and Lucas left.

When they arrived at the Boston train station, Lucas spoke to the ticket agent, telling him that Mr. and Mrs. Bentley had a sleeping car on the eleven o'clock train.

Mr. and Mrs. Bentley...

Since she'd been joined with Lucas in wedded matrimony, her feelings had swung from dazed disbelief to a glimmer of happiness. She'd see her sisters soon. She would travel to Texas married to a man who seemed to care for her in some small way.

Mr. and Mrs. Bentley...

His words echoed in her mind, making her thoughts swirl with confusion but elation too. For some reason her heart thrilled at the sound. When he glanced back over his shoulder, her romantic heart skipped a beat. He had a gentle, teasing side to him that made her feel as giddy as a schoolgirl.

"You boys might need to find an extra car for the train," he told the ticketing agent. "Once you see how many trunks my bride is bringing to Texas."

Lucas winked at her.

My bride...

The Bentley men must have some sort of power of persuasion, she decided. She hung back, while he spoke to the ticket agent. The train idled on the tracks. In a quarter hour they'd board and begin their journey. She patted the paper in her pocket, the list he'd given her. It crackled under her fingers. She reminded herself that he offered a marriage of convenience unless she preferred 'something different.'

"Not likely," she said under her breath.

When they arrived at the train station, he offered to buy her a candied apple. He must have heard about her fondness for sweets. Perhaps Faith and Grace had told him. When she declined, he smirked.

Why had he come for her now, instead of months ago? She'd asked that very question on their way to the station. He gave an off-hand answer, one that she didn't believe. His words made her wonder if he concealed parts of himself behind his amiable demeanor.

Despite his assertion, she felt certain he had some unspoken motive. With his good looks and his swagger, he didn't strike her as the type of man who sought a woman for the sake of love. He was the type who calculated his every move. For some reason, he wanted her, and she had a suspicion he would not have left Boston without her.

They left the trunks with the porters and made their way through the crowds. Hope stopped a few paces from the train cars. The locomotive rumbled further down the track, making the ground beneath her boots quake. Her heart thudded heavily too.

Lucas regarded her with a bemused grin, waiting. When he nodded towards the train, she gave a slight shake of her head. Coaxing a breath into her lungs, she retreated a step.

"I can't leave Boston," she whispered.

His smile faded. "You can't stay."

When she didn't reply, he stepped closer, cupping her shoulders with his hands. "Your bookshop burned down. Some fella's been following you home at night and your landlady tossed you out of her boarding house."

"That was your fault."

He shrugged. "That might be true."

"Might be?"

"What's done is done and now you're coming with me. All you need to decide, *Mrs. Bentley*, is walk or carry?"

"We haven't discussed anything yet. Your ridiculous list, for example."

"All aboard!" the conductor shouted.

Lucas flashed a grin. "My ridiculous list burned in the fire. Poof. Gone up in smoke."

Hope nodded, buying herself a little time to think of a cutting response. The train whistle blasted, making her jump. She bit her lip glancing at the steps leading into the train car, wondering how she, the sensible O'Brian sister, had gotten, well... railroaded into marriage with Lucas Bentley. She patted her pocket, assuring herself the list was tucked away safely.

Lucas lowered to whisper in her ear. "I know I caused a ruckus at the boarding house. It was my fault. I need a wife. You could use a husband. Come with me to Texas. Let me make it up to you, sweetheart."

Chapter Twelve

Lucas

Spending days on end cooped up in a train had been unpleasant enough the first time when he traveled east, but the return trip was even worse. Lucas grew irritable. Falling asleep on a train was about as easy as falling asleep on a runaway horse. Tight quarters and lack of fresh air made it difficult to keep up his charming demeanor.

Their room was comfortable enough, during the daytime. It had a sitting area with two beds on opposite sides, and an adjoining washroom. The ticket had been pricey, but worth it. They traveled in luxury. He should have been as happy as a lark but sharing the tight quarters with his bride made him restless. Not only was he getting tossed about in his berth, he was continually reminded that he shared the tight quarters with a soft, sweet-smelling wife.

Her scent hung in the air. Her belongings, lacy girlish things, took up twice the space of his. Dresses, shawls, gloves. Where would she put all her things when they arrived in Texas? The cabin had two rooms. Two. He didn't have the heart to tell her.

The first night, he washed and put on his pajamas. He emerged from the water closet, hardly able to hold back a smirk. She stood by her bed, regarding him with a stricken expression, clutching her night clothes. He deliberately ignored the swath of lacy material she gripped as if her life depended on it.

"Don't you worry, I'm not going to pounce on you, Mrs. Bentley."

She frowned, hurried past him and shut the washroom door behind herself. He'd never heard a woman getting ready for sleep and was surprised that Hope needed three times as long as he did. Finally, she came out and darted to her bed.

He gave her a moment to get settled. When he thought she might be situated comfortably, he got out of bed, extinguished the gas lamp and drew the curtains. Returning to bed, blindly feeling his way, he considered what, if anything, he should say. Goodnight? Sweet dreams?

It turned out he didn't need to come up with something suitable. Hope spoke before he could.

"When we left Boston this morning, you said you needed a wife, Lucas."

"I do need a wife." He sighed as he sank into the soft bedding. They hadn't discussed the ranch or any of the requirements his uncle had spelled out. She might object to the Clementine clause. In view of her probable displeasure, he'd ease into that subject when the time was right.

She went on, speaking softly. "My mother always said she didn't think my father cared for her. He just married her because he needed a wife to come to America. Her father provided a dowry and money for passage to America."

Lucas wondered where she headed with this topic.

"So, I confess I feel a small bit of happiness to think that you need me, that you felt something for me, and that's why you came all this way."

Her tone made her sound a little lost. He grimaced at her words, relieved he hadn't discussed the deal he'd made with his uncle. Clearly, that would put things in a bad light. The truth was he'd come to Boston to propose, thinking after she saw him in person, she'd set aside her reservations. She'd be grateful for a way to come to Texas. He hadn't imagined how she'd take his breath clean away, or about his desire to, if nothing else, protect her.

The moment he laid eyes on her, he'd fallen hard for her. That was before she'd told him a man followed her at night, and before the bookshop burned down, and before she'd been dismissed from the boarding house, all of which only deepened his resolve to make her his wife. He needed her to claim the ranch, but he needed her because he couldn't bear to leave her alone and defenseless in Boston.

She belonged to him. And truth be told, he belonged to her. He couldn't profess the depth of his feelings, not now. Instead, he went ahead and agreed with her using a deliberately mild tone. "I do care for you, Hope."

It was true. He did care for her, but the simple words didn't come even close to what he felt deep in his heart. Never mind, he told himself. Leave it alone. One day, and he swore it would be one day soon, he'd stand on his new ranchlands, with Hope in his arms, and he'd tell her every single thing that he held so tightly in his heart.

Chapter Thirteen

Hope

Nestled in her berth, Hope awoke to the sound of the train slowing. She blinked and drew a sharp breath when she saw Lucas standing by the window. He was dressed, his hair tidy, mostly, and his beard darkening his jaw a little more than it had yesterday.

"Good morning, Mrs. Bentley."

The simple greeting, said in his usual, gently teasing tone, made her heart well with warmth. With each mile that they traveled, she'd found herself more drawn to him, more aware of his masculine strength and protectiveness. When they'd switched trains in Chicago, he drew her near, shielding her from the attention of male travelers.

"Good morning, Mr. Bentley," she replied, a smile tugging at her lips. She pulled the blankets closer to guard against the morning chill.

"The dining car won't open until lunchtime. I'm going to get off the train and see what sort of food they're hawking at the station."

"Where are we?"

"Kansas City."

"Will you have enough time?"

"I hope so." He grinned. "Don't let them leave without me."

"This doesn't seem prudent."

He pulled on a jacket, straightened his cuffs and shrugged. "My stomach is growling. Kansas City prides itself on its grub. I'm going to get us a basket. I promise to hurry."

A moment later, he was gone. The train slowed, brakes screeching as they rolled into the station. She darted to the window and pulled the curtain shut. While he was out of their cabin, she dressed hurriedly, trying not to fret about the fact that she was alone on the train, and that her husband wandered somewhere out amidst the busy station.

When she was dressed, she pulled the curtains back. She watched the hustle and bustle, searching for a sign of Lucas. Her heart thudded in her chest. The minutes ticked past, making her more fretful with each passing second. The conductor yelled *all aboard*, and she held her breath searching the crowd. Another call from the conductor echoed just as someone knocked at the door.

She cracked the door. Lucas stood outside, a playful smile on his lips. "Breakfast, wife?"

The train lurched.

"You took so long," she cried out.

"Did you miss me, or did you hope I wouldn't make it back in time?"

She frowned at him, threw the door open and stepped aside to allow him entry. He chuckled as he passed, clearly pleased that he'd made her fret. Lucas was impossible. Arrogant, exasperating, and unpredictable. One moment, he would look at her with warmth in his eyes, and the next he'd turn away, clearly determined to keep his distance.

"I was hungry, that's all," she said, trying an aloof tone.

A small table stood beneath the window with a chair on either side. Lucas laid out the food on the linen tablecloth. The aroma wafted through the cabin. Hope's stomach rumbled so loudly, she was sure he must have heard over the clatter of the train wheels.

When he finished unpacking the basket, he held out a chair for her, gesturing gallantly. After she sat down, they bowed their heads as he said a prayer of thanksgiving. They ate their breakfast as the train rolled out of Kansas City. She delighted in the pot of hot tea he'd gotten for her and listened to him describe the various foods. What she called a scone, he called a biscuit. They spent much of breakfast debating the virtues of southern foods and the traditional Irish fare she and her sisters knew.

She felt the familiar warmth come over her heart as she sat across from him, relishing the moments of playful banter. He seemed to enjoy it as well. At one time, amid making a point about Texas fruit orchards, he set his hand over hers and gave her a gentle squeeze.

"I'll be mighty glad to have a wife to come home to at the end of the day," he drawled, gazing out the window.

She blushed, wondering what he meant. They hadn't discussed the details of their marriage. Since getting on the train in Boston, he'd been gentlemanly and tremendously polite. Holding her breath, she waited for him to say more.

"I don't care too much for making my own supper," he finally added.

She blinked. He wanted a wife so he wouldn't have to cook supper? With a lift of her chin, she gave him a level gaze. "Perhaps we can hire someone to cook."

Now it was his turn to appear bewildered. "Hire someone? I thought you were a good cook? That's what Grace said."

She folded her hands before her, trying to hold back a smile. "Ah, now I understand why you made the trip to Boston. To seek out a woman to cook for you."

He fixed his attention firmly on her, neither smiling nor scowling. After a long moment, he reached across the table and took her hand in his once more. This time, he held it in his hand with a gentle clasp and stroked his thumb across the top of hers. Hope stared, transfixed, waiting for him to say something in response to her teasing. Instead, he shook his head and brushed a kiss across her hand.

"I didn't make the trip to Boston to seek a cook. I came for you."

Chapter Fourteen

Lucas

They arrived in Magnolia to be greeted by the growing Bentley clan. Hope stood beside Lucas, clutching his arm as the train wheels screeched beneath them. The racket made it impossible to be heard, so Lucas simply pointed out her sisters at the back of the crowd. They stood beside their husbands, waving excitedly. Thomas and Matt grinned at him as if congratulating him on his success.

As the din of the wheels faded, he bent close to Hope. "They didn't think I'd manage to bring you back. I'll just bet they have a wager going."

Hope laughed softly. "Perhaps my sisters do as well."

He helped her down the steps, holding her hand and shielding her from the crowd. Threading their way through the people, he kept her close, his hand on her lower back. Unsurprisingly, the three women spent some time greeting each other, hugging, laughing, wiping tears of joy. Grace spoke shyly of the baby she expected in a month's time. Faith spoke of her and Thomas's little one, due sometime in the spring.

While the women were all smiles and happiness, Matt and Thomas were more reserved. They introduced themselves to Hope, welcomed her to Magnolia, but behind their friendly smiles, Lucas saw a hint of apprehension. He frowned at them. Neither seemed to want to tell him what troubled them.

After they loaded the luggage and trunks onto the buckboard, Lucas helped Hope up. She gazed around, taking in the sight of the countryside with interest. He could hardly tear his gaze from her and yearned to ask her what she thought. It was absurd. She'd only arrived not twenty minutes ago, yet he wanted to hear that she liked what she saw. Her lips curved into a smile. He'd have to take that as approval. For now.

They drove to the old Bentley homestead, Thomas and Faith's home. There they enjoyed a fine lunch in the dining room. Lucas had grown up eating at the very table. It seemed impossible that he now sat here with his wife, enjoying a meal with his brothers and their spouses.

After lunch he asked Thomas and Matt if he might have a word. They went to the porch, leaving the women in the dining room. Both his brother's expressions grew more troubled as they gathered outside.

Lucas leaned against the railing. "Someone going to spill the beans?"

Matt sighed. "We were going to wait till you'd had a little time to get settled with your bride before we gave you the bad news."

"I can handle bad news and get Hope settled all in one fell swoop. I don't like wondering what sort of bad news you're keeping from me."

"Josh Bentley hired Bing Giddings to contest Uncle Jim's decision. He's determined the ranch should go to him, especially if you don't fulfill the Clementine clause."

Lucas shrugged. "He can't go against what his uncle says."

Matt held up his hands. "Thomas and I have been talking about that very thing. Still, it's worrisome. He might give Uncle Jim a bad time. Jim's getting up in years."

Lucas growled with irritation. "I've spent the last month fixing up the cabin, ordering furniture, and supplies. I had the barn painted and I'm starting on the fencing now to get ready for the Brahma bulls coming in the spring. I did all that because Jim told me it would be mine."

Thomas spoke. "If it falls through, we have a house you and Hope can live in."

"Nothing doing," Lucas said. "Hope and I are keeping the cabin. And the ranch. It's the whole reason I set off to Boston to begin with. Jim said I needed a wife if I wanted to have the thousand acres."

A cry of dismay came from the doorway. Hope stared at him, pale and wide-eyed. "That's why you came to Boston?" Her voice was soft and tremulous. "All because of a ranch?"

Chapter Fifteen

Hope

Thank goodness her sisters hadn't heard Lucas's admission. Hope would never have overcome her mortification if Grace and Faith knew the reason that he'd brought her to Texas was to get his hands on a piece of land.

Both Thomas and Matt looked sheepish. Lucas, on the other hand, gave her a smile, that despite her distress, made her heart flutter. How could a rogue like Lucas Bentley have such power over her? How could her heart betray her? How could she have been so blind to come to Texas after knowing him for such a short amount of time?

The memory of the bookshop's fiery demise came back to her. Following close behind was the way Mrs. Spencer had banished her from the boarding house. She hadn't had many options when Lucas Bentley proposed. Maybe that was because he made sure he was her best choice.

He remained at the railing, motionless, his arms crossed over his chest, leaning against the wooden post. While his brothers both appeared somewhat shame-faced, Lucas didn't show a shred of guilt.

"That wasn't the only reason, darlin'. Besides, when I took one look at you, I knew you were the one for me. The only one for me." He grinned at his brothers. "It was love at first sight. I didn't think it existed. Not till I laid eyes on Hope O'Brian."

Both Thomas and Matt shook their heads, giving her an apologetic look. Matt muttered a few words of warning to Lucas, telling him to quit his teasing.

"I'm not even close to teasing," Lucas shot back. "Come on, Hope. Let's say our goodbyes and I'll show you our little slice of heaven. What do you say?"

She gave him a brittle nod, her mind spinning in turmoil. There was nothing more to say. She followed him back inside, coaxed a smile to her lips and bid her sisters goodbye, with a promise to see them as soon as she'd rested.

"Is everything all right?" Grace asked as they stood by the buckboard.

"It's fine," Hope said, hugging her tightly. "I'm so pleased to see you, but I need to rest a little. The past few days have been almost more excitement than I can bear."

"Help you up, Mrs. Bentley?" Lucas offered.

Hope accepted his help, avoiding his gaze as he lifted her to the bench.

Grace laughed. "Now we have three Mrs. Bentleys."

Lucas nodded. "That's right. Our family's growing."

Thomas, Matt and Faith stood on the porch, waving as Lucas drove the buckboard down the path. Neither of them spoke. Hope kept her gaze fixed firmly in front of her, trying to calm her frantic thoughts. He'd all but tricked her, asking for her hand for personal gain, nothing more.

The path led up a ridge, higher and higher until they reached the top and could see for miles in every direction. The cool winter winds buffeted them, making Hope shiver. Lucas halted the horses and they hung their heads from the effort of the climb. He took off his coat and draped it around her shoulders. She kept her gaze averted but murmured a quiet word of thanks.

The grasses waved in the breeze. Hope drew a deep breath, letting her lungs fill with the clean, crisp air. For the past six days, they'd been confined to a stuffy train compartment except for the times they switched trains. Before that she'd only known the sooty air of Boston. The view from the ridge, the country air, the majesty of the land stretching to the horizon, all soothed her wounded pride, somewhat.

She lifted her hand to her brow, shielding her eyes from the sun's rays. "I suspected you had an ulterior motive when you came to Boston."

"I did," he said gruffly. "But I'm sure that you're better off here with your family. I don't regret what I did. Do you?"

She pressed her lips together, refusing to answer his question.

He snapped the reins.

They continued on their way, Lucas keeping his stony gaze straight ahead, and Hope determined not to answer his question. The wagon creaked, jarring her teeth when the wheels hit a rut. The horses plodded on, unconcerned by their heavy work. They were a pair of matched bays, but nothing like the horses in Boston. Shaggy, big-boned, with hooves the size of pie plates, they were more like draft horses. And the buckboard, with its hard, wooden bench, was no hansom cab.

They approached a grove of trees where a chimney appeared as they drew nearer, and then a second chimney came into view. Hope let out a soft huff of surprise. This was her new home, one she'd share with Lucas. It was a far cry from the Bentley homestead, but very appealing, nonetheless. To her surprise, warmth filled her heart. This was to be their home. A cabin. She smiled.

"We have two rooms, for now," Lucas said as he helped her down.

He held her hand in his. Noting the tone of apology in his voice, she hastened to make it clear she didn't care about the tight quarters. "It's beautiful, Lucas."

He smiled, almost bashfully, making her heart melt. When he lifted her hand and brushed a kiss across her skin, she felt a giddy rush of happiness. She was defenseless against his charms. They walked up the steps hand in hand. The porch wrapped around the two sections of the cabin. Colorful wreaths of greenery and flowers adorned the doors.

Lucas chuckled. "I think your sisters have stopped by while I was away. I ordered furnishings from Magnolia, pots and pans and whatnot, but I didn't think about frilly stuff like those things."

"They're called wreaths," Hope said. "I think you're right. This is the work of my sisters."

"Wonder what other mischief they got into." He led her into the larger of the two rooms. "This is the kitchen, dining area. Pots are new. The table is from the other house."

Hope eyed the table. Scorch marks left by a hot pan marred the top of the table. She ran her fingers over the surface. Despite the imperfections, the table pleased her. Perhaps it was because of the imperfections. The table she had in Boston had been small, of course, with only a single chair. This table could seat six or eight, at least, and the notion of feeding a large, boisterous group of people sent a thrill through her.

"It's not much," Lucas said. "If you don't like it, I can get you something new."

"It's beautiful. Don't get something new. A new one wouldn't have this one's history and..." She paused to think of the right word. "And character."

For some reason her comments seemed to surprise him. He gazed at her for a long moment as if reappraising her. She laughed softly, happy to have been able to change the mood between them. Why she wanted to do that, she couldn't say. By rights, Lucas should apologize, but she sensed he was far too stubborn to tell her he was sorry.

"Let me show you the bedroom," he said.

They walked across what Lucas called the dog-run, a passage between the two rooms constructed to provide a breeze.

"But where are the dogs?" she asked playfully. "I think I'd like a dog, never having had one."

"I'll get you whatever you like, Mrs. Bentley."

Inside the bedroom, the scent of freshly cut lumber filled the air. A half wall divided the room, a bed on one side, and a sitting area by the fireplace on the other side.

"Your sisters made the quilt for the bed, but I'll have you know I made you something too."

He led her to the sitting area. Two rockers sat in front of the fireplace, but what drew her attention was the wall beside the hearth. A set of bookshelves ran the length of the wall, from the floor to the ceiling.

Hope drew a sharp breath. She lifted her hand to her lips and stared at the empty shelves. There was room for scores of books. The wood shone with a brilliant sheen. It was obvious it had just been built and painted.

Lucas ran his hand along the uppermost shelf. "I didn't know you were such a little thing. I reckon I'll need to make you a stepping stool to reach this shelf."

"You built this?" Her voice trembled "For me?"

"I did."

Hope didn't know what to say to that. She hadn't imagined he would do something so kind, so thoughtful. Her gaze drifted from Lucas to the shelves and back to Lucas.

"I figured you might like a place to read, and a place for your books," he said quietly. "I wanted to give you both of those things as a wedding present."

Chapter Sixteen

Lucas

Coming home in the evenings filled his heart with a satisfaction he hadn't expected. He spent his days building fences in preparation for the cattle that would come in a few weeks' time. While he worked in the fields with the other Bentley ranch hands, Hope kept busy in the cabin.

Each evening, when he walked up to the house, he was greeted by the aroma of the dinner she'd prepared. He'd kick off his boots, untie his chaps, and hang up his spurs, leaving his belongings outside in the breezeway. He'd step inside to find her busy with dinner and making their cabin a home.

At night, he'd lie awake, listening to her soft breathing on the other side of the bed. In ten days of being married to Hope, he'd kissed her only once, and that had been in Boston. While she sassed and teased and joked with him during the day, she was shy and reticent at night.

In addition, she was exhausted. She worked as hard as he did, cooking, cleaning, running into Magnolia with Matt's cook, Mrs. Patchwell, and learning how to manage a Texas household. One day, he returned for dinner and found her asleep in the rocker, a half-peeled potato in her hand. She'd been mortified that she didn't have supper ready. He dismissed her fretting and peeled the potatoes for her, while she attended to the rest of the meal.

One day, when he worked alone digging fence posts, he heard her call his name. He looked up to see her at the top of the pasture, a basket in her hand. She waved to him and made her way through the long, waving grasses. She wore a bonnet, but her hair had fallen loose and blew in the breeze. Unabashedly, he stared, wondering how he'd managed to find such a lovely girl.

"I brought you a sandwich and some lemonade," she said.

"That's mighty sweet of you," he said. "I should do something nice for you."

She set the basket on the buckboard and took out the sandwiches, wrapped in linen. "Like what?"

He leaned against the buckboard, eyeing her soft, copper ringlets, wondering if they were as soft as they looked. "I could take you fishing."

She laughed. "I've never been fishing before."

"We should take a day off. On Sunday a traveling preacher will be passing through Magnolia. What do you say we go to church? After, we can do a little fishing. Maybe have fish for lunch."

"Where would we go?" she asked.

"The stream between our place and the other Bentley property."

She knit her brow. "Faith and Grace will be back from Houston on Sunday. They've invited us to supper. I've hardly seen them since I arrived in Texas. Will we still have time for both?"

"We'll just go for a spell."

With a smile tugging on her lips, she nodded. "All right. Sounds fine to me."

Sunday morning dawned, and he heated water for a bath while Hope slept. He washed and dressed and heated more water for her bath. He left the cabin to hitch the horses and bring the buckboard. When she emerged from the house, she wore a blue dress that made her eyes look even bluer.

"You look beautiful," he told her.

She smiled. Her cheeks pinked. They drove into Magnolia, to the small chapel where services were held. The preacher gave a stirring sermon about God's plan for his children. Lucas felt the message keenly in his own heart and wondered what Hope's thoughts were on the subject.

Later that afternoon, as they walked the short distance to the river, he asked her. "I'm sure you expected something different when you agreed to come to Texas."

She looked up at him, a questioning expression in her eyes. "How so?"

"The cabin isn't near as fancy as your sisters' homes."

"Did you think I needed something fancy?" She gave him a playful pat on his shoulder. "Thomas told Faith you thought I was spoiled because I'm the youngest."

He grimaced. He'd forgotten he said that some time back. "I don't think you're spoiled."

She was anything but spoiled. She was pretty and sweet, and filled a spot in his heart he hadn't realized was empty. At night, when she slept and he lay awake, staring at the ceiling, he thought of the tender words he'd like to say to her, but during the day they'd vanished from his mind.

"You don't think I'm spoiled!" She laughed. "How kind of you, Mr. Bentley. Tell me, are you the type of man who gets upset if his wife catches more fish than he does?"

He snorted. "Hope, you've never even held a fishing rod. You probably won't catch anything today."

Her smile widened. Her eyes sparked with mischief and he'd never wanted to kiss her more. He imagined pulling her into his arms and kissing her right there on the riverbank. He resisted the powerful urge. He knew nothing about wooing a woman, but he imagined a first, real kiss should involve sweet words, moonlight and such.

Instead, he prepared the hooks and cast the pole for Hope. When he finished, he shucked his boots and waded out into the stream with his pole. The cool water chilled his skin. His feet slipped a time or two on the smooth river rocks. Hope would have a good laugh if he tumbled into the shallow river. Thankfully, he made it to the middle of the stream without mishap.

The river brought back memories from his childhood. Along with his brothers, he'd come here countless times to swim and fish. On those days, they'd work fast, leaving some daylight at the end of the day for a few hours of fun. They'd finish their chores early, and their mother would prepare them a dinner basket and send them down to the river. They'd spend the evenings here, until the stars peeped from the darkening sky, and return home in the moonlight, tired and happy.

He was pleased to share this spot with Hope even if she'd never fished before. Over the next hour, he had to return to the bank three times to put fresh bait on her hook.

"If you feel a tug, it's probably a fish," he teased.

She gave him a prim look. "Thank you. I intend to catch a bigger fish than you."

He grinned. "We'll see about that. I intend to catch a fine bass and fry it up for my lunch."

"What about my lunch?"

"I'm not sure what you'll have for lunch if you keep on feeding the worms to the fish."

He returned to the middle of the stream, cast his rod and was rewarded with a hard pull on the line. He whooped, set the hook and began reeling in his line. The fish gave him quite a fight, but in the end Lucas won. He held up his prize as he returned to shore.

Once he strung the fish on the stringer, he went back out to the stream. Standing in the middle of the stream, surrounded by the sparkling waters, he couldn't resist a few teasing comments about Hope's lack of success. She sat on the bank, perched on a rock. She lifted her chin and gave faint smiles, but she refused to respond.

A short while later, she called out to him. "I believe I'll return to the cabin. I'd like to make a pie to take to my sisters for dinner."

He couldn't help feeling disappointed she was leaving. He'd enjoyed the afternoon more than he realized. Maybe it was because he'd teased her. She gave him an impertinent look prompting him to give one, final teasing remark. "All right, play your cards right, I might let you have a little of my fish."

She shook her head with disapproval, but he didn't miss the curve of her lips. The time at the river hadn't proved to be the romantic outing he'd hoped, but he'd enjoyed it immensely, nonetheless. He stayed a short while longer, trying to catch another fish, but found no luck.

He didn't care to remain at the river without Hope, so with a sigh, he returned to the riverbank. He gathered the bait bucket, the poles and finally went to the spot where he'd left the fish. To his surprise, the stringer along with the fish had vanished. He peered into the water, chuckling. "Why, you little thief," he said under his breath.

Chapter Seventeen

Hope

Hope very nearly stumbled as she hurried along the trail with her pilfered loot. She wasn't exactly sure where the reckless notion had come from, but something about Lucas's smirk inspired her to a small, well-timed payback. She hadn't anticipated it would be so difficult to sneak away with his prize.

When Lucas had boasted about his fish, he claimed it weighed five pounds. With all the thrashing, the fish felt like it weighed far more. Lucas also said the bass was *a real beauty*. Hurrying back to the cabin, Hope decided the fish was hardly beautiful. Despite being out of breath from the effort of lugging the creature back to the cabin, she giggled at her own mischievousness.

This wasn't the first time he'd teased her or made jokes at her expense. In Boston, he'd played a trick or two on her too. It was high time for him to have a taste of his own medicine. She set the fish down on the grass and hastily pumped water into a bucket. Then she plopped the fish in the water. It thrashed about, splashing her with its tail. Pausing for a moment, she admired his silvery-gold fins and the speckled markings running along the curve of his back.

She'd eaten fish in Boston, of course, but her family bought fish from the fishmonger. This creature looked quite different than the offerings in the fishmonger's stall. She admired the way the sun glinted off his scales. Maybe, as Lucas said, this fish was a beauty. The fish sank to the depths of the bucket. She sprang into action. Eager to conceal her tracks, she set the bucket behind the cabin.

Her heart raced.

Would he be the sort of man who grew angry when teased?

She'd been too young to recall many of her father's rages, but she'd heard enough about them from Faith and Grace. With a shiver, she wondered if perhaps she'd acted rashly. What was done was done, she decided, and set about making her pie dough.

The minutes ticked past. Hope could hardly contain her nervousness as she waited. Every so often, she left her task and peeked out the window to search for Lucas, but he didn't appear. Was he still fishing? Had he noticed that the fish was missing?

Setting the pie in the oven, she went to the door, intending to wait for him outside. She opened the door. Lucas stood on the threshold. With a shriek, she whirled and ran back inside. He entered, closed the door and leaned against it, his arms folded. His expression was inscrutable.

Edging away from him, she gave a breathless laugh. "Any more luck fishing, Mr. Bentley?"

"No, Mrs. Bentley," he said slowly. "You might say my luck vanished."

"I'm so sorry to hear that. It couldn't happen to a nicer, more humble person."

His lips quirked. He crossed the kitchen, closing the distance between them. Hope backed against the counter, scarcely able to draw breath. He drew close. The corners of his lips tugged into the hint of a smile. He kept his dark gaze firmly fixed on hers. When he stood so close, she had to look almost straight up to meet his eye.

"Something you want to tell me, Mrs. Bentley?"

She swallowed hard. "Yes, Mr. Bentley. You're very tall."

He nodded, clasped her waist, and with a quick, effortless motion set her on the counter. She gasped in surprise. In the few weeks they'd been together, he'd never been so forward. His gaze drifted down to her lips and then slowly returned to her eyes.

"Is this better?" he asked.

"For what?" she whispered.

He smiled, stroking her jaw with his thumb. "Hope, you're so beautiful."

She laughed softly. "As beautiful as a five-pound bass?"

"Even more beautiful than a five-pound bass," he said with a chuckle. "And sassy too."

"Sometimes I like to sass my husband, just a little."

"I always like it," he said softly. "I think God meant for us to be together."

Her eyes widened. "I never know..."

"Go on, sweetheart. Tell me."

"Sometimes I'm not sure where the Lord wants me. But I'm trying my best."

"Hope," his voice broke from emotion, and his restraint gave way.

He cupped her face, lifted her chin and kissed her. The kiss was soft and tender. When he wrapped her in his arms, she felt the warmth of his passionate embrace. She'd never imagined a kiss could steal her breath. She yearned for the kiss to never end. Sinking into his strong arms, she gave herself over to his touch.

Chapter Eighteen

Lucas

That afternoon, Lucas and Hope made the short trip to Grace and Matt's home. They ate an early supper, retiring afterward to the front porch. The sun sank in the western sky, casting a soft glow across the porch, and the three sisters chatted as they sat together on a bench.

Lucas and his brothers, along with his nephew, Caleb, gathered on the other side of the porch to discuss ranch plans and business. Lucas only half-listened. Mostly he kept his gaze on his wife, sitting between her sisters. The three women studied a swath of lace that Faith had made for a christening gown. He smiled, noting the different shades of red hair, and the way they chattered, their voices brimming with happiness.

"I heard you went fishing this afternoon," Thomas said.

The words pulled Lucas from his reverie. "Fishing?"

Thomas frowned. "Could have sworn that's what Hope said."

Caleb nodded. "That's what I heard too. She told us that you caught a nice bass."

Lucas cleared his throat. "That's right."

"But then you lost it," Caleb said. "Slipped off the hook?"

Lucas shook his head. "Not exactly."

The boy knit his brow. "He snapped the line?"

"You're mighty interested in this fish," Lucas grumbled.

Thomas smirked. "I heard someone made off with it."

Lucas shook his head, raking his fingers through his hair. "News spreads fast around here."

Caleb's eyes grew big as plums. "Somebody stole your fish, Uncle Lucas? What did you do to him?"

Lucas felt his face warm. The memory of taking Hope in his arms and kissing her rushed back with a wave of happiness, along with a small measure of embarrassment. He certainly didn't want to tell his brothers and young nephew what he'd shared with Hope, their first real kiss, but judging by the smirks on his brothers' faces, they'd guessed as much.

"Well, Caleb, I'm sorry to say it was your Aunt Hope who stole my fish," Lucas said a little louder than necessary. Hope lifted her gaze to meet his, a lovely pink blossoming across her fair skin.

Caleb's mouth fell open. Thomas and Matt chuckled along with Hope's sisters.

"Probably a misunderstanding," Lucas added.

Hope smiled. "Nothing of the sort. The fish was filched because Lucas had boasted all morning about his skills, suggesting I'd have no lunch if I didn't catch something."

"Did you both get to have lunch?" Caleb asked. "Or did you keep it all to yourself?"

"Course I shared with her. What do you take me for?" Lucas asked. No one answered his question, all of them regarding him with a look of bemusement.

"We had a little Texas fish fry," he said.

Mrs. Patchwell, Matt and Grace's cook, called Caleb in to help clear the table. After he left, Thomas turned to Lucas with a more serious expression. He spoke quietly. "Did you tell Hope about Uncle Jim's demand?"

Matt nodded. "Does she know about the Clementine clause?"

"Not exactly," Lucas said. "I aim to, though. Soon."

His brothers gave him disbelieving looks.

"What if Jim comes around?" Matt asked. "Or Josh?"

Lucas growled softly, displeased that his brothers hounded him with questions. He tried to dismiss any more questions from his brothers, and to forget the concerned looks etched around their eyes. Shortly, Mrs. Patchwell called them in for dessert and coffee. After Lucas ate several slices of pie and cake, and Hope had enjoyed her sweets, Lucas told the family it was time he and Hope were on their way.

They drove home as the sun slipped past distant hills, painting the horizon a brilliant crimson. The sky dimmed from a brilliant, cloudless blue into a deep shade of purple. As the nightfall darkened the land, stars twinkled overhead.

Maybe it was nothing more than wishful thinking, but Lucas imagined that she sat a little closer to him than she had on the way over. On occasion, her shoulder would brush against his. Each time, he had to suppress the urge to drape his arm around her and draw her even nearer. He imagined what it might feel like to fall asleep with her resting her head on his shoulder.

Hope admired the lovely night sky as they turned for home. Her sighs and words of wonder distracted him. He found himself stealing admiring looks at his lovely bride.

"I've never seen so many stars," she marveled. "What with the lamplights and sooty air, we can hardly catch sight of the sky, never mind the stars."

"It's a good thing you agreed to come to Texas, isn't it?" he asked, his voice a little gruffer than usual.

She gave him a playful pat on his arm. "All along, I was quite certain I had no choice in the matter. You threatened to carry me off like some sort of barbarian."

Her laughter, lighthearted, and full of joy, drew an answering laugh from him.

"In regard to your question," she went on, eyes lifted to the sky, "I am very happy to be here with you, Mr. Bentley, to admire the night sky. I'm certain I've never, in all my life, seen anything so beautiful."

He nodded, watching her as she spoke, the last rays of dusk lighting her face. "Neither have I, Mrs. Bentley."

Chapter Nineteen

Hope

The dark moments before dawn were Hope's favorite time of the day. A peaceful hush lay over the cabin and the surrounding land. When she drew water from the well, she'd stay outside for a spell, relishing the quiet.

If she lingered a little longer, she'd hear the first signs of day's awakening. A bird, perched in the pecan tree, chirped. Another bird, some distance away, gave an answering call, and soon the countryside sprang to life as the sun lit the eastern horizon.

A few days after dinner at Grace and Matt's home, Lucas saddled his horse before the sun rose, intending to help his brothers. The three men needed to tend to a windmill on the far side of the ranch. Hope offered to pack food for the men. Lucas thanked her but refused. Mrs. Patchwell, the cook, would bring lunch.

"I'll send Caleb over to help you with your chores," Lucas said.

"I can manage, although I'd welcome the company. I'll make a pie."

Lucas grinned. "Save some for me."

With that he kissed her goodbye and rode off. Hope spent the morning tidying the house. She washed several of Lucas's shirts, sewed a button on one of them, and made a pie for

Caleb. Late morning, she heard the approach of a horse and buggy, and, assuming it was the boy, went to the porch to wait.

To her surprise, two men drove down the path. A rather portly gentleman, dressed in fine suit, drove a horse that looked more like a Boston thoroughbred than a Texas ranch horse. Another man rode with him, taller, younger, with a hard look about him. He looked as though he was more at home in the saddle than in a buggy.

A covey of quail alighted. The horse snorted and side-stepped. The driver chuckled and soothed his horse with gentle words.

"Now, Reginald, no need to show off for Mrs. Bentley," he said with a grin.

The driver didn't seem like much of a threat, but Hope hung back just the same, feeling somewhat vulnerable without Lucas nearby. She nodded politely, not wanting to give offense. "Good day, gentlemen. May I help you?"

The driver took off his hat, revealing his thinning hair. "My name's Bing Giddings, Mrs. Bentley. I'm an attorney-at-law. This here is Josh Bentley, cousin to your husband and brothers-in-law."

The younger man nodded but didn't smile. Despite his unfriendly demeanor, she saw the family resemblance. It eased her mind somewhat. The unsmiling man might be a stranger, but he was a Bentley.

The driver, Bing, went on. "I had the pleasure of meeting your sister, Faith, when she first arrived in town."

His tone, full of charm but with a hint of mischief too, made her smile. She recalled the stories of when Faith came to Magnolia. "What exactly do you mean by that, Mr. Giddings?" she asked with a hint of amusement in her voice.

She wondered if Lucas's cousin had heard the story of Faith being duped by a bank robber. He arched a brow and listened intently, his lips tugging upward.

Mr. Giddings cleared his throat and gave her a solemn look. "I'm sorry to say that Sheriff Bentley detained me in the town jail that morning. It seems I'd overindulged in spirits the evening before and caused some trouble in town."

Josh chuckled, making Hope think this behavior was common knowledge. Mr. Giddings reddened and frowned at him before going on.

"It's a terrible habit, ma'am. I can assure you it only happens once a year. The rest of the time I'm the most well-mannered man in Magnolia."

Hope could see what the confession cost the poor man. In addition to the flush on his skin, beads of perspiration glistened on his receding hairline. He blotted his brow with a linen handkerchief.

"Just once a year?" Hope prompted.

"Yes, ma'am. The anniversary of my poor wife's death."

Hope felt a pang of regret, wishing she hadn't asked. "Oh, dear. I am sorry."

"I don't mean to burden you with my sad tale." He tucked his handkerchief in his pocket. "I wondered if Mr. Bentley and I could ask you a few questions about your nuptials with Lucas Bentley."

Hope grew wary. "My husband's not home at the moment."

"Perhaps we could sit on the porch. It won't take but a minute."

"I'm making a pie for Caleb. I expect him any moment."

"Would you mind if we waited? We promise not to cause you any trouble or inconvenience."

"We'd be much obliged." Josh spoke at last in a deep voice that reminded her of Matt's.

Hope debated. She didn't know the men, but it would be bad manners to turn them away. She was certain that Josh was who he said he was, so she agreed. "All right."

"Much obliged," Josh said, disembarking from the buggy. "We'll just wait out here."

"What is that heavenly aroma?" Mr. Giddings asked as he clambered down.

She frowned, not sure what she thought of the pair of men, arriving unannounced, requesting pie. Despite her misgivings, she returned to the cabin, took the pie from the oven and served them both a slice along with a cup of coffee.

Sitting on the bench next to hers, Mr. Giddings thanked her several times over. He ate slowly, complimenting her on her baking. Hope sat on the edge of the bench, acutely aware of how untoward the situation was, but brimming with curiosity. What sort of questions did they have about Lucas?

Josh said little, devouring the pie hungrily as if he hadn't eaten in some while. He looked hale and hardy, but hungry too. She offered him more, but he declined.

When Mr. Giddings finished his pie and coffee, she took the dishes inside and returned to the porch. By that time, Mr. Giddings had retrieved papers from his buggy. He wandered back to the bench, shuffling through the documents, muttering under his breath. Josh leaned against the railing. His attention wandered over the cabin and further out to the pastures as if studying her and Lucas's property.

"Ah, yes! Here we go. Now I apologize for the indelicate question, but I must ask, first off, are you and Mr. Bentley married?"

Hope felt her face warm. "Yes, sir. We married in Boston before we came to Texas. Would you like to see the pastor's certificate?"

"No, ma'am. Your word is enough."

The tension in her shoulders eased.

"I know your sisters are good people and assume you're of the same moral fiber."

"I'd like to think so."

Mr. Giddings tapped the papers on his knee in an attempt to collect them neatly.

Hope smiled despite the lingering awkwardness. "Is that all?"

"I only have one other question. It's a silly one at that. It's regarding the Clementine clause."

"What?"

Mr. Giddings scanned the papers, running his finger down each sheet. "Says here that Lucas Bentley agrees to marry within two months, and that was six weeks ago, so we're fine there. And when or if the good Lord should bless you with a girl child, the Clementine clause requires that she shall be named Clementine."

"The Clementine clause." Hope's voice was barely above a whisper.

"Lucas didn't mention that?"

"No." Her words came out a little stronger this time.

"Mrs. Bentley, I regret to inform you, the Clementine clause is part of the contract."

Josh regarded her with a mixture of pity and bewilderment. For the life of her, Hope couldn't imagine why he had come with the lawyer to inquire about such personal matters.

She schooled her features to hide her astonishment. All along she'd been certain Lucas had held back some small part of the agreement, and now she knew. She wouldn't make a fuss, not now, not with two strangers on her porch, but later, when he returned, she'd demand to know every aspect of the contract. As his wife, she was certain she was entitled.

Hoofbeats drummed down the path, drawing her attention from Mr. Giddings. Caleb galloped toward the cabin. Dust billowed behind them. In an instant, she was on her feet, hurrying to the rail. The boy slowed to a canter when he saw her, but it was clear he was highly distressed. When he reached the cabin, he pulled his horse up.

"Aunt Grace is in trouble. The baby's coming. Nobody's there to help her and she says she can't do it alone."

"Merciful heavens," Hope whispered.

The boy's eyes shone, brimming with tears. "She's hurting. I didn't know where Uncle Matt and the others are working."

Hope gave a small cry of dismay. "What on earth am I to do? I don't know anything about-"

Without a word, Josh untied the horse. Mr. Giddings, pale and clearly alarmed, crossed the porch with surprising alacrity. He took her arm and gently led her to his buggy. "Come with me and Josh, Mrs. Bentley. We shall take you to your dear sister."

Chapter Twenty

Lucas

In the past, all Lucas ever wanted at the end of the day was to sink into a hot tub. With a wife waiting at home, he had relished the idea of a long soak in mind and spending the evening with Hope. All day long, he'd missed her something fierce.

Riding up the ridge, he scanned the distance for a plume of chimney smoke that always greeted him, the telltale sign she worked on supper. His stomach rumbled. Mrs. Patchwell had delivered sandwiches, boiled eggs and apples, along with a fine lemon cake, but that was six hours ago. He was ready to eat.

And more importantly, he was ready to be home with his wife.

He'd been away from her for darned near twelve hours. He laughed at his own foolishness. Twelve hours was nothing, really, in a man's life. But these twelve hours away from his sweetheart seemed like an eternity. If his brothers knew he'd been counting the hours till quitting time, they would have had a good laugh. He'd always been the Bentley brother who claimed he didn't need a pesky wife. Now look at him. He was like a love-sick boy.

At the top of the ridge, he urged his horse into a trot. When the house came into view, his heart skipped a beat. Something was wrong. The kitchen door hung open. Not even a wisp of smoke rose from the chimney. The house was empty.

Hope wasn't there.

Despite that certainty, he cantered to the cabin, dismounted and raced inside. Calling her name, he strode from room to room. When he finished searching inside, he ran back out and checked the outbuildings. It wasn't like her to go to the barn, but just the same, he looked there anyway, and in the shed too.

He returned to his horse, mounted and cantered down to the stream where they'd fished only a few days before. Trotting along the banks, he found no footprints. He breathed a sigh of relief. She hadn't come to the river.

The only other possibility was that she'd left with someone, or she'd been taken. He pushed the thought aside. That kind of trouble couldn't happen here in Magnolia. He wouldn't allow himself to think of anything so terrible. And yet, as he rode back to the cabin, fearful possibilities formed inside his mind.

Dear God, keep her safe. I'd give up anything...

As he neared the cabin, he saw the tracks of a wagon. On closer inspection, he could tell the tracks were from a buggy. The tracks led in the direction of Matt and Grace's home. He put his horse into a gallop. Tearing down the path, he crouched low in the saddle. His horse thundered along the well-worn trail. They raced, the wind blowing the horse's mane and making tears stream down Lucas's face.

Matt's horse was hitched to the rail in front of the house. Bing Giddings stood outside, chatting with Caleb and Thomas, and smiling. When Bing caught sight of Lucas, he waved. Standing beside Bing was another man. Lucas recognized his cousin, Josh, and swore under his breath.

"It's fine," Bing shouted. "Just fine. The baby's well and so is Grace."

Lucas slid from the saddle. Caleb hurried over and took the reins from him.

"Is Hope here?" he demanded, his voice cracking with emotion. "Tell me she's here."

"She's here," Thomas said, clapping him on the shoulder. "Bing brought her. Thank goodness she was able to come."

"What happened?"

Thomas shook his head. "You're not going to believe this. Hope delivered her own nephew."

Lucas took the steps two at a time and rushed inside. He wanted to call for her but resisted the urge. A baby had just been born. It wouldn't be fitting to holler inside the home and disrupt the quiet. Fortunately, he found his wife almost at once. She came to the top of the stairs. Her hands flew to her cheeks. She pressed her lips together and blinked back the tears that threatened to fall.

"Lucas," she whispered. "I'm so glad to see you."

He charged up the stairs, forgetting all about staying quiet. When he reached the top, he swept her into his arms, and held her tighter than he'd ever held her. "Sweetheart, you gave me a scare."

"I did?"

"I couldn't find you. I thought someone had stolen my girl."

"I'm sorry. I didn't think. There wasn't any time. Grace needed me."

"Of course, sweetheart." He set her down. "The baby is okay?"

She gave him a tearful smile. "He's fine. And beautiful. He looks just like his daddy."

Lucas wiped his thumb across her cheek to dry her tears. "Isn't that something. And to think you were the one to help bring that little fella into the world. My sweet and precious Hope."

Chapter Twenty-One

Hope

The light of late evening sunshine softened as the sun sank in the sky. Hope had never felt so tired. She'd stayed by Grace throughout the day as her sister labored. After the baby was born, Hope cleaned and diapered him, dressed him in a soft, warm gown and swaddled him in a blanket. To her astonishment, Grace seemed remarkably animated. She gazed down at her son, her eyes lit with joy, chattering about the baby's mouth, so like Matt's, and his blond hair, so like their mother's golden locks.

It had been a long day, and Hope was ready to go home.

Matt sat on the side of the bed, his expression still a little dazed. The doctor had sworn Grace still had time. He was certain her time was still a few weeks away and Matt had assumed the same.

"I just can't believe it," Matt muttered. "I'm so sorry I wasn't here, darlin'."

"It's all right," Grace murmured, giving her husband a loving look.

Abigail, their daughter, drew close to the bed and frowned at the newborn. "He needs a name. Poor baby."

"I know, Abigail. Here I had all sorts of girls' names picked out, and our early arrival turns out to be a boy. I suppose I'll need my Abigail's help to name her brother."

The young girl beamed. Pride lit her face. Matt chuckled and drew her into his embrace.

"I'm going to let you rest," Hope said, kissing Grace on her forehead.

Grace drew a sharp breath, her eyes shining with emotion. "I don't know what I would have done if you hadn't come."

Hope brushed off her words. When she'd arrived, Grace was very close to giving birth. She lay in bed, moaning softly. It was clear that she was exhausted. Hope sprang into action. With a few words of encouragement from Hope, Grace managed to deliver the baby.

The poor child was born listless and hardly breathing. Hope recalled from a book she'd read long ago how newborns responded to vigorous strokes along their limbs. Unsure of what to do, she'd done the only thing she could think of, and, by some miracle, the little one cried out, plaintively at first, and then more loudly. In no time, he protested with noisy, forceful wails. Hope smiled as she recollected the way the infant yelled, almost indignantly.

Hope looked down at the sleeping infant. His fair lashes fanned across his rosy cheeks. His small mouth worked small movements that made both her and Grace laugh.

"Such an angel," Hope said. "I should let you rest. And I need to too. I'm so tired. Lucas is too. He was very worried when he came home, and I wasn't there. We'll be over early tomorrow to see if you need anything." She circled the bed, embraced Matt and Abigail and said her goodbyes.

Matt embraced her, tears in his eyes and spoke, quietly. "Thank you so much, Hope. Lucas is on the porch waiting for you. I've never seen him like that, like he'd just lost everything that matters. Please give him my apologies for giving him such a scare."

Hope felt a rush of warmth. It felt like ages since she'd said goodbye to Lucas that morning. So much had changed in the course of a single day. She lingered to give the baby one final look, marveling at the small miracle nestled in Grace's arms.

The boy's birth had moved her in ways she couldn't describe. Amidst fear and wonder and awe, the small child had made his way into the world, a little early perhaps, but in retrospect, all had unfolded with God's perfect timing. She would never forget witnessing the baby's arrival, or the look in Grace's eyes when she first glimpsed her son.

Hope paused in the doorway to drink in one last look of the new child and his parents. For as long as she could recall, she'd wondered where her place was in the world. A soft warmth fell over her heart. It was here, in Magnolia, amongst her sisters, and their families, and at Lucas's side. That's where she belonged. The realization came over her with a gentle but undeniable certainty.

She stepped out of the room, shutting the door softly behind herself.

Lucas waited for her outside. He greeted her with a smile and a kiss. "You delivered a baby."

"I still can hardly believe it," she marveled. "He's the sweetest little child. A perfect miracle."

His expression sobered. "I heard there was trouble and that you revived the boy."

She brushed his words aside. "I was happy to help in any small way."

He nodded, his gaze never wavering. "One day, God willing, we'll have a few of our own."

She was about to say something about that topic, when to her astonishment, he declared he would carry her home on his horse, seated in front of him. With a gasp, she searched the barnyard for Mr. Giddings with his fancy buggy, or even Caleb, who might be persuaded to hitch horses to a buckboard. But there was no one.

A moment later, Lucas mounted on his horse, swept her into his arms and turned towards their cabin. The horse seemed entirely unperturbed by the notion of transporting two people. Hope, on the other hand, could hardly believe she rode alongside her husband. It was quite unseemly, although she had to admit, she relished his arms around her. Fortunately, they rode along a desolate country path.

"This is an outrage, Mr. Bentley," she announced, feigning indignation.

"I think it's perfect, Mrs. Bentley."

Lucas kissed her hair and tightened his hold on her. Held against him, she both felt and heard the rumble of laughter deep in chest. She pressed her lips together as she recalled her conversation with Mr. Bing Giddings.

"And speaking of outrages..."

He glanced down at her, his eyes sparking with amusement. "Here we go. I suppose Bing and Josh told you about the Clementine clause."

She rubbed her finger along his jaw and spoke quietly. "My father only married my mother so that he could gain passage to Boston. I don't like being part of a bargain."

"I am sorry."

"Wh-what?" She hadn't imagined Lucas Bentley would apologize so easily.

His smile had faded. He looked at her with a solemn expression. "I am very sorry, Hope. I wish I'd been straight with you from the beginning."

Her husband, she decided, looked very handsome when he apologized. She swallowed hard, trying to dislodge the lump in her throat. With a quick nod of her head, she shrugged off the issue, hoping they might change the subject altogether. Suddenly, the issue didn't seem so important anymore.

"You deserved better," he said gruffly.

"Lucas," she said quietly. "Please, let's not speak any more of it."

He drew a deep sigh. "When I couldn't find you this afternoon, I realized that none of this land matters, not the pastures, not the cabin. Nothing. I love you, Hope, and none of this has any meaning to me if I don't have you by my side."

His gentle, soft-spoken words cast a welcome warmth across her skin. She laid her head against his chest and sighed, a deep sigh of contentment. "I love you too, Mr. Bentley. So very much."

He kissed the top of her head. "You'd better love me, Mrs. Bentley."

The sky darkened as the sun slipped below the horizon. The evening stars twinkled in heavens. They arrived at the cabin, just as the brow of the moon crested the eastern hills. The silvery light cast a lovely glow over the land.

That evening, Hope prepared for bed, donning a gown and brushing her hair. Lucas entered the room as she finished braiding her hair. He smiled, letting his gaze linger on her reflection. He unbuttoned his shirt and tossed it over a nearby chair. Firelight flickered from the grate where a blaze crackled. The glow lit his handsome features.

"About that Clementine clause," Hope said softly. "What if we never have children?"

"You mean if I keep staying on my side of the bed, and you keep staying on yours?"

Warmth blossomed across her skin, crawling across her neck and heating her cheeks. "What I mean is that not all couples have children. Jim and Ernestine didn't have any little ones."

Lucas rubbed his jaw thoughtfully. "Maybe we'll adopt. Take in a needy child."

She rose from the chair, crossed the room in her bare feet and stopped before him. Her heart drummed against her ribs. Her knees felt weak, making her sway unsteadily. Lucas frowned and pulled her into his arms.

"Are you all right sweetheart? You had quite a day."

"I'm fine," she whispered. "I suppose I feel just the same as your uncle."

"What do you mean by that?"

She gave a breathless laugh and hoped her courage wouldn't fail her now. "I mean that I'd like nothing better than a little girl named Clementine."

Lucas chuckled and stroked her hair. "Why, Mrs. Bentley. You surprise me."

"Or a little boy," she said wistfully. "Either would be a blessing, don't you think?"

"I do," he said quietly. "Either a little boy or a girl would be a blessing, indeed." He lifted her chin, brushed a kiss across her lips. "Or both a boy *and* a girl." His lips quirked with a mischievous smile, the same playful smile she'd grown to love so very much.

Epilogue

Lucas

Mark Bentley was well on his way to being more of a scamp than his father or uncles. Of that, Lucas was certain. The five-year-old clung to the top branches of the pecan tree, his younger brother, four-year-old Silas, clambered on the branches below, trying valiantly to reach Mark.

"Get yourselves down here before you tear your good trousers," Lucas called to the boys.

Mark looked affronted. "I was a good boy just like you told me. I sat through the baptism and made Silas stay quiet too."

"You said we could play a spell, Pa." Silas hung from a branch, swinging by his arms.

"I didn't mean climbing the pecan tree like a pair of monkeys."

Both boys snickered.

"Just a few minutes more, Pa." Silas gave him a pleading look, one that always worked wonders with his mother.

"What's that on your knee, son?"

"Sir?"

"That green stripe. You ran off to play not two minutes ago and you already got a grass stain on your trousers. What's your mama going to say about that?"

Silas swung to a lower branch. He landed with ease, but Lucas's stomach churned to see his boy so high in the tree.

Mark perched even higher, but his eldest son had more experience climbing the old pecan.

"Mama's not going to fuss," Silas said. "She only fusses when we clobber each other."

Mark grinned and snickered at his brother. "You mean when I clobber *you*."

Silas glared up at his brother and raised his fist. "I clobber you plenty!"

"I don't care who clobbers who," Lucas thundered. "I'm going to clobber the two of you if you don't get down here now."

This of course, was a mostly empty threat. Lucas disciplined the boys when they needed correction, but thankfully, that was a rare occurrence. They were fine boys, he had to admit, despite his irritation. The way to handle boys, he'd come to realize, was to keep them busy and wear them out. Both Silas and Mark worked with him on the small tasks they could manage. Sweeping, painting, tending to the livestock.

That method didn't do much good on a day like today, the baptism of his and Hope's third child.

"Serves you right, you know."

Lucas turned to find Mrs. Patchwell standing behind him, a grin on her face.

"It's only fair you have children who were as incorrigible as you were."

There was no denying her words. "God help me," he muttered.

"I'll get them down," she said.

"Doubtful."

"Gentlemen," Mrs. Patchwell called.

"Yes, ma'am." Both boys answered in unison.

"What a pair of little lambs," she said under her breath. "Must be the O'Brien influence."

Lucas rubbed the back of his neck. "Don't get your hopes up, Mrs. Patchwell. They're usually very good at minding their elders, but both of them are tired of sitting and being cooped up."

"I've baked three different desserts," Mrs. Patchwell called. She sniffed. "Your auntie baked two more."

"Aunt Grace?" Mark asked, his voice brimming with excitement. "Did she make her chocolate cake?"

Mrs. Patchwell grumbled. "I believe so."

Both boys whooped.

She frowned at their outburst. "I made blueberry pie, lemon chiffon and my strawberry cake. The cake that won first place two years in a row at the county fair."

She rattled off the various treats, but she needn't have bothered. Both boys climbed down the tree as if their life depended on it. The mention of Grace's chocolate cake provided all the incentive they needed to leave their fun and race to the family table as quickly as they could.

Lucas and Mrs. Patchwell followed them, walking up the hill side-by-side.

"Mrs. Bentley does make a fine chocolate cake. I'll grant her that," Mrs. Patchwell said, her voice tinged with resentment. "Shame she didn't win first prize, isn't it?"

Lucas grinned. "You're famous for your baking, Harriet. Thank you for making this day even more special."

Her lips tugged upwards. "I wouldn't have missed it for the world."

The dining room, just off the kitchen, had been built the year before. The table seated all of the Bentley clan, but at the rate their numbers were growing, might not accommodate all of them in the years to come.

Hope sat to the right of his chair at the head of the table. She held their newborn as he slept. When she looked up and smiled at him, his heart skipped a beat, his breath caught, and he stopped in his tracks. They shared a long, lingering gaze full of warmth and love. The way his wife looked at him was always a balm to his soul.

Grace and Faith hurried to and fro, bringing heaping platters of meats, and bowls brimming with side dishes. The children sat amongst the adults. Josh Bentley had come for the baptism too. He had made the trip from his ranch south of Magnolia. Sitting across from Matt, he debated the cost of beef and horse feed.

Josh looked up as Lucas crossed the dining room, heading to his seat. "You know you still haven't fulfilled the Clementine clause, don't you Lucas?"

Matt and Thomas laughed. Caleb, sitting beside his father, joined in. Even Mrs. Patchwell, working in the kitchen, chuckled at Josh's teasing comment.

In the years since Lucas and his brothers had married, not one had been blessed with a daughter. Matt had four boys. Thomas had three, Caleb and two youngsters. Lucas and Hope had three sons of their own.

Lucas circled the table and kissed his wife. "My beautiful, Hope," he whispered. He paused a moment to gaze down at their youngest, Henry, born two weeks prior. The infant slept peacefully, nestled in his mother's arms. Lucas would have liked to take the child in his arms but didn't want to disturb the boy's slumber.

He sat down and nodded Caleb's direction. "It might be up to Caleb to have a girl child."

Caleb turned red, making everyone laugh. "I'm only sixteen, Uncle Lucas."

Lucas turned to his uncle, seated at the opposite end of the table. "You hear that Uncle Jim?"

His uncle leaned forward and cupped his ear. "Eh?"

Lucas spoke a little louder. "Young Caleb might have to find himself a wife so we can take care of the Clementine clause."

Uncle Jim waved his hand and knit his bushy brows. He jerked his thumb Josh's direction. "This fella needs a wife. It would do him a world of good."

Josh shook his head. "No disrespect, sir, but I'm not looking for matrimony. I already had my heart stomped on once."

"Bah!" Uncle Jim grumbled.

Lucas grinned. "Uncle Jim, will you lead us in prayer?"

His uncle grimaced. "I don't like my meat rare!"

Lucas pressed his hands together in a gesture meant to suggest prayer.

Uncle Jim's laughter boomed across the table. Young Henry startled and whimpered but settled when Hope soothed him with a soft word. The family, both young and old, bent their heads, clasped hands and joined the elder Bentley in a prayer of thanksgiving.

The End

Book Five of Mail Order Bluebonnet Brides
Mail Order Destiny

Magnolia, Texas, 1880's
A jaded, wealthy rancher. A desperate mail order bride.

Sophia McSweeney needs to escape the dangerous slums of
Boston. When she accepts Josh Bentley's marriage offer, she
seeks safety, not love. She sets out for Texas and prays her
husband can forgive her past. She dares to hope for redemption.
She never expects a man who makes her heart soar.

Josh Bentley is no stranger to heartache.
Josh has no use for romance. He vows to take a wife that
understands her role. A helpmeet that will stand by his side and
do her part to run his family's ranch.

Books by Charlotte Dearing

<u>The Bluebonnet Brides Collection</u>
Mail Order Grace
Mail Order Rescue
Mail Order Faith
Mail Order Hope
Mail Order Destiny

<u>Brides of Bethany Springs Series</u>
To Charm a Scarred Cowboy
Kiss of the Texas Maverick
Vow of the Texas Cowboy
The Accidental Mail Order Bride
Starry-Eyed Mail Order Bride
An Inconvenient Mail Order Bride
Amelia's Storm

Mail Order Providence
Mail Order Sarah
Mail Order Ruth

and many others...

Sign up at <u>www.charlottedearing.com</u> to be notified of special offers and announcements.

Printed in Great Britain
by Amazon

. 39643480R00067